a fairy's fire

For editors Christy and Chris.
Thanks for everything. —K.T.
For my sister Angela, who is a superstar. —J.C.

Library of Congress Cataloging-in-Publication Data is available upon request.

ISBN 978-0-7364-3556-7 (trade) — ISBN 978-0-7364-8175-5 (lib. bdg.) — ISBN 978-0-7364-3557-4 (ebook)

randomhousekids.com
Printed in the United States of America
10 9 8 7 6 5 4 3

Disney
The Never Girls

a fairy's fire

written by
Kiki Thorpe

illustrated by
Jana Christy

A STEPPING STONE BOOK™
RANDOM HOUSE 🏠 NEW YORK

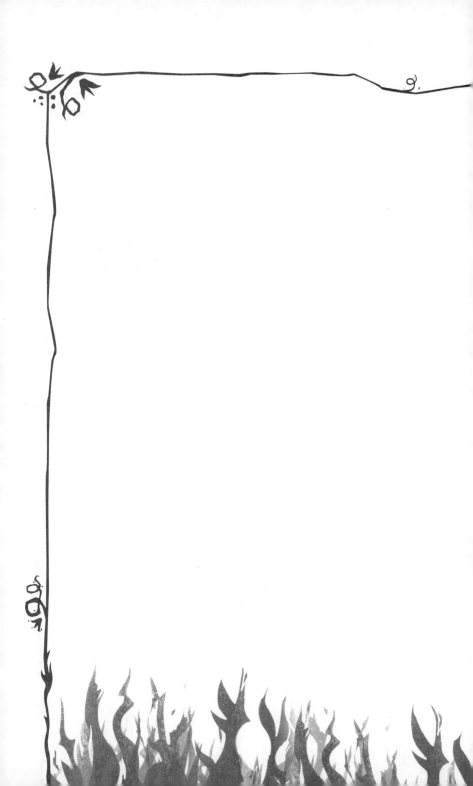

Never Land

Far away from the world we know, on the distant seas of dreams, lies an island called Never Land. It is a place full of magic, where mermaids sing, fairies play, and children never grow up. Adventures happen every day, and anything is possible.

There are two ways to reach Never Land. One is to find the island yourself. The other is for it to find you. Finding Never Land on your own takes a lot of luck and a pinch of fairy dust. Even then, you will only find the island if it wants to be found.

Every once in a while, Never Land drifts close to our world . . . so close a fairy's laugh slips through. And every once in an even longer while, Never Land opens its doors to a special few. Believing in magic and fairies from the bottom of your heart can make the extraordinary happen. If you suddenly hear tiny bells or feel a sea breeze where there is no sea, pay careful attention. Never Land may be close by. You could find yourself there in the blink of an eye.

One day, four special girls came to Never Land in just this way. This is their story.

Never Land

Pirate Cove

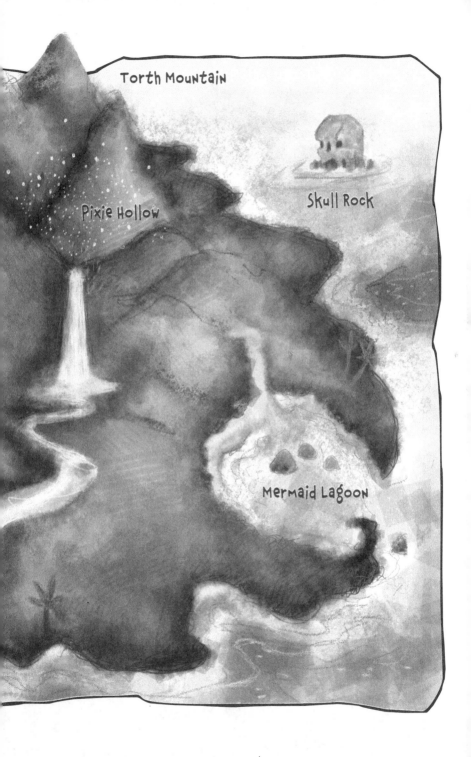

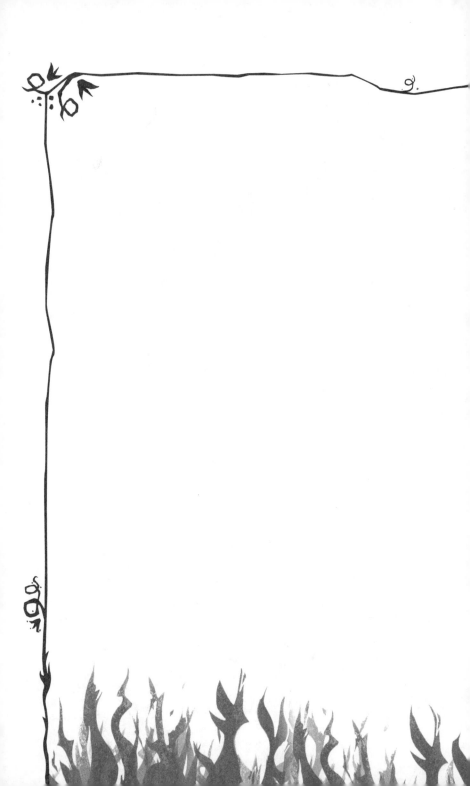

Chapter 1

Kate McCrady stared out her living room window, her arms folded across her chest. A moving van was parked in front of the house across the street. She watched as movers unloaded furniture from the house and carried it into the truck.

"I can't believe it. The Johnsons are moving?" asked Kate's best friend Mia Vasquez.

Kate nodded glumly. The Johnsons had lived across the street for as long as she could remember.

Her other best friend, Lainey Winters, pushed her glasses up her nose and peered at the moving van. "Where are they going?"

"To Florida."

"Florida?" said Lainey. "That's so far away!"

"I know," Kate said unhappily. "They told my mom that they'd always wanted to move there. But they didn't plan to go so soon. Some people offered them a lot of money for their house. That's why they're leaving now."

"That stinks," Lainey said sympathetically.

"Well, maybe the people who move in will be nice," Mia suggested.

"There's no way they'll be as nice as the

Johnsons," Kate grumbled with a scowl.

Kate loved the Johnsons as if they were her grandparents. The older couple was always doing nice things, like bringing Kate cookies on her birthday, which they always remembered. And they had always been there to help. When Kate fell off her bike, Mrs. Johnson had cleaned up her scraped knees *and* given her a bowl of mint chocolate chip ice cream. And the time Kate locked herself out of the house, Mr. Johnson had let her read his old comic-book collection until her parents got home.

Now they'll be baking cookies for some kids in Florida, Kate thought.

Just then, Mr. and Mrs. Johnson came out of the house. Mr. Johnson was carrying a suitcase. Mrs. Johnson had a large bag over her shoulder. They stopped to talk to one of the movers.

"Do you want to go say good-bye?" Mia asked Kate.

Kate shook her head. She had said good-bye to her neighbors the day before. She was afraid if she talked to them now, she would cry. "I have a better idea," she said, turning away from the window. "Let's go to Never Land."

"What about Gabby?" Lainey asked.

They all knew they had to wait for Mia's little sister. When the friends had discovered a magical portal to Never Land in Mia's backyard, Gabby had been with them. The four had made a pact to always go together.

Mia checked the clock on the wall. "She

4

should be home from dance class by now."

"Then what are we waiting for?" Kate started for the door with her two friends close behind. Her heart felt lighter with each step. *Everything will be better in Never Land,* Kate thought. Nothing ever changed on the magical island. No one ever grew up or grew older or moved away.

And that was just how Kate liked it.

A short time later, Kate, Mia, Lainey, and Gabby wiggled through the loose board in Mia and Gabby's backyard fence, where the portal to Never Land was hidden. Even as she crouched at the hole, Kate could smell the sweet scent of orange blossoms and the salty sea air. A warm breeze fluttered the ends of her hair. She stepped through into bright sunlight and smiled.

Pixie Hollow was buzzing with activity. A trio of harvest-talent fairies, each carrying a freshly picked plum, darted through the trees. Garden-talent fairies fussed over flowers, coaxing them to stand taller on their stems. A flurry of leaf-boats carrying water fairies passed on Havendish Stream.

Something is happening, Kate thought. She could sense excitement in the air. "I wonder— Whoa!" Kate ducked as a pair of swallows zipped past, narrowly missing her head.

Beck and Fawn, the two fairies riding the birds, looked back over their shoulders.

"Oops! We'd fly backward!" Beck called out. That was how fairies apologize.

"Busy day today!" Fawn added as they swooped away.

"What's going on?" Lainey wondered.

Downstream, Kate spotted a sparrow man emerging from the double doors of the mill. "There's Terence," she said. "Let's ask him!"

The girls hurried along the banks until they reached the little building made of peach pits. Next to it, a wooden water wheel turned briskly in the stream.

Kate raised her voice to be heard over the splashing. "Fly with you, Terence! What's happening? Why is everyone so busy?"

"Haven't you heard?" Terence replied. He darted around, checking the levels of fairy dust in the great pumpkin canisters where it was stored. When he flew down into one, his voice echoed from inside. "A fairy is arriving!"

"Arriving from where?" Mia asked.

Terence popped his head up. His hat sparkled with fairy dust. "You know. *Arriving.*"

The girls looked at him blankly. Terence's eyes widened. "Don't tell me you don't know where fairies come from?"

"I guess I never thought about it," Kate admitted.

"You mean, a new fairy is going to be born?" Gabby asked.

Terence laughed. "In a manner of speaking, yes. And lucky you, you'll be there to meet her."

"Oh!" Gabby's face lit up with delight.

"Afraid I can't talk right now, though,"

Terence told them. "Lots to do. Lots to do. A new fairy is arriving, and it just might be a dust talent. . . ." His voice grew muffled as he disappeared into another canister.

As they walked away from the mill, Gabby couldn't contain her excitement. "A new fairy! I wonder what kind it will be? And where do they come from? Are they babies when they arrive? How come we haven't seen baby fairies before? Do you think they'll let me hold it?"

"I don't *know,* Gabby," Mia said, laughing. "Let's find someone else to ask."

The girls started toward the Home Tree, the giant maple that was the heart of the fairies' world. As they got closer, Kate saw that it looked especially grand today. Firefly lanterns hung from every twig. The windows had all been washed until they sparkled, and sweeping-talent fairies were busy cleaning the steps that wound around the base of the trunk.

In the courtyard, tiny tables held a fairy feast of roasted chestnuts, acorn bread, sliced berries, candied violet petals, and other delights. The girls spied a freckled fairy in a rose-petal dress hovering among them.

"Prilla!" Kate and her friends called in unison. Prilla was the first fairy they'd ever met. She was also the one who'd first brought them to Pixie Hollow.

Gabby rushed over to her, asking, "Will they let me hold the baby?"

"Baby?" Prilla asked.

"She means the new fairy," Mia explained.

Prilla grinned. "So you've heard the news!

The laugh should be here any moment. The scouts have been watching it ever since it got to Never Land."

Now Kate was really confused. "What do you mean, the *laugh*?"

"The laugh that will become the fairy, of course," Prilla explained. "When a human baby laughs for the very first time, the laugh flies out into the world and turns into a fairy."

"Oh!" Kate felt a nervous fluttering in her stomach. She had the sense that she was about to witness something especially magical.

"I'm really glad we came today," Mia said, as if reading Kate's mind.

"It's not every day you get to see an arrival,"

Prilla agreed. "A new fairy is cause for rejoicing. That's why everyone is working so hard. We don't yet know what talent the new fairy will have. All the talent groups want to honor a new member with their very best work."

Gabby, who had been examining a table full of penny-sized cakes, looked up at Prilla. "But *how* does a laugh turn into a fairy?"

"You're about to find out," Prilla said, darting into the air. "Look!"

"I don't see anything," said Kate. But then she did. There was a wrinkle in the bright blue of the sky, as if the air there was concentrated. It was moving rapidly toward them.

"Is that it?" Lainey whispered.

"Yes!" Prilla replied.

All around them, the sound of soft

fluttering filled the air. Hundreds of fairies were emerging from the nearby woods, meadows, and stream. The fairies landed all around the courtyard, murmuring in anticipation.

Just then, the great knothole door in the Home Tree opened. Queen Clarion floated down the steps and took her place near the front of the crowd.

The laugh had reached the Home Tree. The crowd seemed to hold its breath as the laugh drifted downward. As it came closer, it began to spin, picking up speed. It flashed and sparkled.

Down, down, down it came. The laugh lightly touched the ground—and the grass around it suddenly burst into flames!

Chapter 2

The water fairy Silvermist was watching from the edge of the crowd, when she saw the grass catch fire. She jumped back, startled. *Where did that come from?*

The other fairies seemed stunned, too. They stared as the fire quickly spread across the grass, heading toward the roots of the Home Tree. Silvermist's friend Tinker Bell bumped her shoulder. "Silvermist! The water!"

"Oh!" Silvermist looked down at the full bucket in her hands, a welcoming gift in case the new fairy was a water talent. She darted over to a patch of burning grass and tossed the water onto the flames. They went out with a sizzle. Only a pile of smoldering ashes and a thin trail of gray smoke remained.

"Over here!" Kate hollered. She was stomping on a row of burning buttercups.

"Rani! Marina!" Silvermist called to two more water fairies. They snatched dewdrops from a nearby mulberry bush and pelted the fire with them. At the edge of the courtyard, two cooking-talent fairies tipped a cauldron of soup onto the last of the flames.

With the fire safely out, Silvermist looked

around at the damage. Patches of burned grass and flowers dotted the area, but at least no one was hurt. Silvermist grimaced at the smell of smoke lingering in the air. As a water fairy, there was nothing she hated more than fire.

"Ashes and dust! I'm all wet!" someone exclaimed.

Everyone turned. In all the commotion,

they'd forgotten about the arrival! The new fairy was standing in the middle of the courtyard, examining her dress, which was soaked.

The new fairy suddenly seemed to notice that everyone was staring at her. She lifted her head. Her eyes were startling. They were black as coal, but at the same time bright, as if a spark shone in them.

Gabby's loud whisper broke the silence. "She's not a baby fairy at all. She's just regular size."

"Shhh!" Mia hushed her younger sister. "She's so pretty, though!"

She is *striking,* Silvermist thought. Her strange, dark eyes were rimmed with long lashes. And her flaming red hair fell almost to her ankles.

The new fairy's wings unfurled, fluttered once . . . twice . . . then extended to their full length. Terence flew forward, reached into his satchel, and carefully measured out a teacup full of dust. He sprinkled it over the new fairy, as was customary. The moment the dust touched her, the fairy began to glow— first lemon yellow, then bright gold, which deepened to reddish amber.

The crowd murmured in surprise. "Have you ever seen a fairy with a red glow?" Tink whispered.

Silvermist shook her head. Everything about this arrival was odd, right down to the fairy's garment. She looked as if she were wrapped in wisps of smoke.

The new fairy didn't seem to notice anything strange. She smiled around warmly. "Fly with you," she greeted the crowd. "I'm Necia."

A hush fell. Every fairy in Pixie Hollow leaned forward. Here was the moment they'd all been waiting for—the new arrival was about to announce her talent.

But the fairy said nothing.

"And your talent, dear?" Queen Clarion prompted.

Necia looked at her with mild surprise. "Fire," she said, as if it were obvious.

What? Silvermist leaned over to Tink. "There's no such thing as a fire talent . . . is there?"

"Not that I've ever heard," Tink said.

Queen Clarion gave a little shake of her

head, as if she hadn't heard correctly. "Did you say *fire*?" she asked.

"Yes, *fire*." Necia snapped her fingers, and a spark appeared. When she cupped her hands around it, the spark leaped into a flame. The fire danced across Necia's fingers, growing bigger and bigger, until it seemed to cover her whole hand.

Silvermist gasped. *She'll be burned alive!* Thinking quickly, she snatched a pot of tea from a nearby table and threw the contents at Necia. The fire hissed out.

Necia turned on Silvermist. "What did you do that for?" she spluttered, wiping tea from her face. Her dress was stained, and her glow had turned even redder.

"What do you mean?" Silvermist asked. "I saved you! You were on fire!"

"I was *holding* fire," Necia corrected her.

"But I thought . . . I thought . . . ," Silvermist stammered. What had she done wrong? Hadn't Necia been in trouble? How could she *hold* fire without getting burned?

Tinker Bell spoke up. "It's just that there's never been a fire-talent fairy in Pixie Hollow before," she explained to Necia. "Silvermist thought you were in danger."

"Never been a fire talent . . ." Surprise replaced the anger on Necia's face. She turned to Queen Clarion. "You mean, I'm the only one?"

The queen nodded.

"Oh." Necia gazed again at the awestruck faces, as if she couldn't quite believe it was true. When her eyes reached Silvermist, Necia paused.

A cold shock ran through Silvermist. The new fairy was glaring at her!

"Well," Queen Clarion said smoothly. "Let's show Necia to her room so she can change into fresh clothes. We can come back to the courtyard and celebrate later."

Slowly, the crowd broke up. A few decorating- and sewing-talent fairies guided Necia to her room in the Home Tree. The rest went back to their work.

Rani, another water-talent fairy, came over to Silvermist. "Are you okay?"

"Yes." Silvermist gave a little laugh, trying to shake off the bad feeling. "Though I don't think the new fairy likes me very much," she added.

"I'm sure that's not true. It was just a misunderstanding," Rani said.

"Of course," Silvermist agreed. "A mis-understanding."

But as she flew off in the direction of Havendish Stream, a feeling of uneasiness came over her again. She couldn't stop thinking about the look Necia had given her. It had been a look of pure poison.

Chapter 3

"That was definitely the *coolest* thing I've ever seen!" Kate exclaimed. She grabbed onto a branch over her head and dangled, monkey-like, swinging her legs. "When the fire just *burst* out of her hand? So awesome!"

It was a beautiful afternoon. Kate and her friends had decided to go for a walk while they waited for the arrival celebration to start. The woods around Pixie Hollow were covered in wildflowers. Birdsong echoed through the trees. Leaves rustled in the warm breeze.

"I thought that part was kind of scary," Mia said. "I don't really blame Silvermist for throwing that tea on her."

"Prilla told me most arrivals aren't like that," Lainey said. "Usually the fairy just appears and announces her talent. Nothing catches on fire."

"Well, *I* wasn't scared," Gabby said. "I thought it was neat!" She reached up and grabbed a low branch, swinging like Kate.

Kate laughed. She gave one last kick and launched herself off the branch. "Come on!" she called to her friends, skipping ahead. Her heart felt light with possibility. They had all day to play in Never Land, and a fairy party to look forward to, and—

Kate stopped short. In front of her was a patch of scorched earth, maybe five or six feet wide. The area had burned to the ground. All that was left was a dusting of gray ash and the charred skeletons of a few bushes. A hint of smoke hung in the air.

Kate knelt and hovered her hand just above the ground. To her surprise, it was still warm. "Do you think this has something to do with Necia?" she asked.

The other girls crowded around to inspect the burned area. "The laugh that made her could have passed through here. Maybe it caused a few small fires on the way?" Lainey suggested.

"It's a good thing it didn't spread," Mia

said. "Imagine if there was a forest fire."

Kate shuddered. She didn't want to think of what could happen to Pixie Hollow in a fire. "We should tell someone. I mean, what if the laugh started other fires?"

"You're right, we should go now." Mia turned and started back the way they'd come. But she'd only gone a few paces, when she stopped suddenly. Kate, who was right behind, almost bumped into her.

Mia was looking at something on the ground near her feet.

"What is it?" Kate asked.

Mia pointed to a set of tracks in the dirt. They were unlike any animal tracks Kate had ever seen—long and narrow, with skinny toes. *They look almost like handprints,* she thought, though she'd never seen a human hand that big. Each print was topped with a row of deep claw marks.

"What animal made these?" Kate wondered.

"A bear?" Mia guessed.

Lainey spent a lot of time with the animal-talent fairies. She knew more about animals than the other three girls put together. She knelt and adjusted her glasses. "No, I don't think so. They're longer than bear tracks.

And narrower," she explained.

"What about a rhinoceros?" Gabby asked.

Lainey shook her head. "Rhinos have three toes. The animal that made these tracks has four. And from what I can tell, some pretty long toenails." She stood and brushed the dirt from her knees. "We should ask Fawn. She'll know."

Mia looked around the woods. "Do you think whatever made it is still nearby?"

"I doubt it," Lainey said. "The fire would have scared any animals off. Come on."

The girls started back the way they had come, ducking under vines and climbing over fallen tree trunks. Their walks in the Never forest were never straightforward, since the only trails were the ones made by deer.

"Shouldn't we be in Pixie Hollow by now?" Lainey said after a while.

The girls looked around. Just when Kate was starting to think they were lost, Mia spied a familiar clump of red toadstools. Before long, the Home Tree came into view.

They found the animal fairy Fawn up in a nearby sycamore tree. She was cleaning the swallow she'd been riding earlier, brushing its feathers to a glossy shine. When the girls called to her, she sent the bird off and flew down to greet them.

"Quite a day it's been so far!" Fawn said with a grin. "First an arrival, then a fire. What next?"

"We're hoping *you* can tell us," Kate said.

"What do you mean?" Fawn asked.

"We found tracks in the woods. Big ones!" Gabby exclaimed. "Kind of scary-looking, too."

"We thought you might know what animal made them," Lainey added.

As Lainey began to describe the tracks they'd found, a strange expression came over Fawn's face. "Those sound like dragon tracks!"

Kate's stomach did a little flip. "Did you say *dragon* tracks?"

Fawn nodded.

"There's a dragon in Never Land?" Kate repeated. "A *real* dragon?"

"Yes," Fawn said. She was twisting the end of her braid around and around nervously. "His name is Kyto."

Never Land was full of surprises. But

Kate was amazed that the fairies had never mentioned this particular one. "Why didn't anyone ever tell us before? I can't believe there's been a dragon here this whole time and we never knew it!" she exclaimed.

"Me either," said Mia. She looked a little pale.

"I suppose no one thought to tell you," Fawn said. "Kyto is chained to a rock near the base of Torth Mountain. He hasn't bothered anyone for ages."

"Phew!" Lainey sighed. "Well, that's a relief!"

"At least, he *was* chained to a rock," Fawn continued. "But if what you saw really were dragon tracks . . ." She trailed off.

"You mean, he could have escaped?" Mia yelped.

"I don't know," Fawn said, but she looked worried. "I'd better see those tracks."

Mia frowned. "Do you think it's really a good idea to go back into the forest now?" she asked. "I mean, with a dragon on the—"

"I'll take you!" Kate interrupted, cutting Mia off. She wasn't afraid of any dragon. In fact, she couldn't think of a more exciting adventure! "Come on."

Kate plunged back into the forest, with Fawn close behind. After a moment's hesitation, the other girls followed.

As they walked, Kate peppered Fawn with questions about Kyto: Was he big? Did he breathe fire? Did he lay eggs? Had anyone ever battled him before? Fawn gave one-word answers to her questions—yes, yes, no, yes—but she wouldn't say more.

"You said Kyto was chained up," Kate pressed. "Who chained him?"

"We did, of course. The fairies," Fawn replied.

"How?" asked Kate.

"When?" asked Mia.

"Why?" asked Lainey.

Fawn heaved a sigh. She seemed to realize that they wouldn't stop asking questions until she explained. "No one knows why Kyto came here. Some think he just wanted a place to nest. Others say he came looking for items for his hoard."

"His hoard?" asked Mia.

"His treasure hoard," Fawn explained. "Dragons collect valuable things. The rarer the object, the better. Maybe there are some that collect peacefully, I don't know. But Kyto was a terror to Never Land. When he roamed free, no one was safe. He'd take what he wanted. And he'd eat whatever—or *who*ever—he liked."

"Even fairies?" Gabby asked in horror.

"If he could catch them," Fawn said with a nod. "He was cunning and malicious, too. He'd ruin things just out of spite. So the fairies came up with a plan. We made a silver collar and a chain to catch him. It took all our magic to trick him into it. This happened some time ago."

Kate knew better than to ask how long. When fairies said "some time ago," it could mean one year or one hundred. It was all the same to fairies. For them, time stood still.

"But you don't chain up other animals, even if they're dangerous," Lainey pointed out.

"Kyto isn't like other animals," Fawn told her. "He's cruel. His heart is full of hate. He'd burn everything in Pixie Hollow to a crisp just for fun."

Gabby stopped walking and looked at her. "Could he do that?"

"Of course he could." Fawn stopped, too, and looked around impatiently. "Where are these tracks?"

"Just over there," Kate said. "By that big tree, I think. Or . . . maybe they were that way? Near those ferns?"

Kate turned in a circle. But nothing in the forest looked familiar. She had no idea where the tracks were. Lainey, Mia, and

Gabby were no help. No one could remember exactly which way they'd gone.

The girls and Fawn searched for hours. But they couldn't find the tracks. At last, Fawn threw up her hands. "We're wasting time. I have to tell Queen Clarion. If there *is* any chance Kyto escaped, she'll know what to do."

They started back toward Pixie Hollow, with Fawn leading the way. Soon the woods began to thin. Kate could see Havendish Stream ahead. On the far bank, a group of fairies stood watching something.

"The celebration must be about to start!" Mia said.

They saw a flash of light. "It's Necia," Gabby exclaimed. "Oh! Look what she's doing!"

Across the stream, Necia was coaxing a flame into a ball of fire. She moved her hands apart, and the fireball grew bigger and bigger.

Gabby broke into a run. "Necia! Wait! I want to see, too!"

Necia's head snapped up. The sight of Gabby—a giant girl in costume wings and a pink tutu bearing down on her—must have startled the new fairy. She wobbled and lost her balance. The fire slipped from her grasp.

Oh no! Kate inhaled sharply. The grass ignited in a *whoosh* and a blaze of light. Fire quickly spread along the banks of the stream, propelled by the summer breeze.

"Help!" cried Terence. The fire was headed right for the mill!

Chapter 4

Silvermist was paddling her birch-bark canoe down Havendish Stream, when she heard the shouts. Clouds of smoke filled the air. She turned and saw fire blanketing one bank.

"Help! The fairy dust!" a voice called out.

Through the haze, Silvermist saw dust-talent fairies and sparrow men throwing bucketfuls of water on the fire. It seemed to be doing little good. The fire was only inches away from the mill. In moments, the bins of fairy dust would go up in flames.

Silvermist dropped her paddle and plunged her arms into the stream. She swirled her hands, using all her water magic to summon a wave. The water swelled beneath her, rising, rising. . . .

The wave crashed onto the shore. Instantly, the flames died out.

"Nice work, Silvermist!" someone cried.

Other water fairies were flying in from other parts of the stream. Silvermist landed next to them on the bank. Smoke had blackened the side of the mill, but the wall remained solid. The dust was safe. The same couldn't be said for the area around

it, though. The grassy meadow was scarred with black.

Terence was sitting nearby, looking dazed.

"Terence," Silvermist said, flying over to him. "Are you all right? What happened?"

"I'm not sure," he said in a shaky voice. "Necia was showing us her fire talent, and—"

"Showing *off* is more like it," a sneering voice broke in.

Silvermist looked up. She wasn't surprised to see Vidia hovering above them. The fast-flying fairy was always ready with a cutting remark.

"You're one to talk about showing off, Vidia," Silvermist replied. Vidia always loved to prove she was the fastest.

But Vidia's usual smirk was gone. Her pale face had gone white with fury.

"She almost burned down the mill—and all the dust with it. Where would that have left us?"

Silvermist knew why she was so angry. Without dust, Vidia couldn't fly—not fast, anyway. Without fairy dust, their talents didn't amount to much. Fairy dust was what gave them their magic.

"*I* once took just a bit of extra dust without asking," Vidia went on, "and I was grounded for days. Necia almost sent the whole stock-pile up in smoke. How will *she* be punished?"

"I'm sure Queen Clarion will do what she thinks best," Silvermist said.

Still, she thought, Vidia had a point. Necia had some explaining to do.

"Where *is* Necia?" asked Terence.

They all looked around. Silvermist suddenly realized the fire fairy had disappeared.

"Fleeing the scene of the crime, no doubt," Vidia snarled.

Silvermist frowned. "That's enough, Vidia."

But still she felt a flash of anger. Was Vidia right? Had Necia run off? Where was her sense of responsibility?

Silvermist was beginning to wonder why anyone would have a talent for fire at all. So far, it had only caused trouble.

Just then, Silvermist spied her friend Fawn hurrying past. Silvermist flew over to her.

"Have you seen Necia?"

"No. Why do you ask?" Fawn replied. She was fiddling with her braid the way she did when she was upset.

"Why? The fire, of course! She almost burned down the mill—and all the fairy dust with it—and no one has seen her since. She flew off, just like that!" Silvermist huffed.

"Necia is the least of our problems," Fawn told her. She lowered her voice to a whisper. "Kyto might be loose."

Silvermist stared at her friend as the words sank in. "How do you know?"

"The Clumsy girls found some tracks in the forest," Fawn replied. "From the sound of it, they might have been dragon tracks."

Silvermist gasped. "You think he escaped?"

Fawn nodded. "Yes, maybe." She looked around at the other fairies. "I don't want to upset anyone until we know for sure. I'm going to tell the queen now."

"I'm coming with you," Silvermist decided.

Necia's whereabouts could wait, for the moment. If what Fawn said was true, they had bigger things to worry about.

Inside the Home Tree, Silvermist and Fawn flew up the circular staircase to the second floor. They paused outside Queen Clarion's chambers. The door was slightly ajar. They could hear someone talking.

"Should we knock?" Fawn asked.

As Silvermist reached out to rap on the door, the voices spilled out into the hallway. She peered around the edge of the door. There was Necia, having a private meeting with the queen.

So that's *where she's been!* Silvermist thought. She'd been wrong about the new fairy. Necia hadn't run away from the fire. She'd gone directly to the queen.

Just then, the queen raised her voice. Silvermist caught the words ". . . you need supervision. A water fairy, perhaps. Just until you can control your talent."

"I *can* control it!" Necia exclaimed. "I was surprised by that Clumsy, that's all. If she hadn't run up, it never would have happened."

Silvermist backed away from the door. "We should leave," she told Fawn. She knew they shouldn't be listening to the conversation.

"I'm not going anywhere. I need to tell the queen about Kyto!" Fawn insisted.

"All right." Silvermist pushed the door closed. But the queen's voice still came through.

"Necia," Queen Clarion said gently, "I know this is disappointing, but I've made up my mind."

There was a moment of silence. Then came a quiet reply. "Yes, Queen Clarion."

A moment later, the door swung wide. Necia exited the queen's chambers. Her head was down. But she looked up sharply when she saw Silvermist and Fawn.

"You were *listening*?" Her eyes burned Silvermist with accusation.

Silvermist opened her mouth to reply, then closed it. What could she say? She *had* been listening, even if she hadn't meant to. A knot formed in the pit of her stomach. If Necia hadn't liked her before, she was going to despise her now.

Necia gave a snort of disgust, then shouldered past her and continued down the hall.

"Silvermist, come on," Fawn said. She was already halfway inside the queen's room. Silvermist hurried after her.

"Queen Clarion?" Fawn said as they entered. "We need to speak with you urgently."

"Oh, good. You're here," the queen replied. "I need to speak with you, too." The queen adjusted her crown and floated down a few steps to the center of the room. "Necia told me all about the fire at the mill. I understand it was an accident, and she is quite remorseful. Still, it put Pixie Hollow in great jeopardy. Silvermist, we have you and the other water fairies to thank for saving the fairy dust. You acted very bravely."

Silvermist bowed her head slightly. "It was nothing, Queen Clarion."

"As you know," the queen continued, "Necia is a new fairy. She's still learning how best to use her talent, as all new fairies must. However, I have given it thought, and in light of today's events, I think she needs supervision. We can't afford any more accidents."

Silvermist nodded. "Queen Clarion, I couldn't agree more—"

"I'd like you to stay close to her for a

while, Silvermist," the queen said.

"Me?" Silvermist exclaimed.

The queen nodded. "If another accidental fire starts, I'll feel better knowing you're there."

"But, Queen Clarion, isn't there . . . *anyone* else?" How could she explain that Necia already didn't like her, and this would only make things worse? Besides, the thought of being near another fire—the heat, the smoke, the horrible crackling—made Silvermist feel queasy.

"I think it's clear that you're the best fairy for the job," the queen declared.

Silvermist nodded, but her heart sank. She couldn't think of anything worse than looking after the fire fairy.

The queen smiled and turned to Fawn,

who had been fidgeting impatiently. "Now, what did you want to tell me?"

"Queen Clarion," Fawn said, "we think Kyto may have escaped."

As Fawn explained what the girls had told her, the queen's smile faded. She began to pace around the room.

"Did you see these tracks yourself?" the queen asked.

"No," Fawn admitted. "The Clumsies couldn't find them again. But I can't think of any other animal with a track like the one they described."

"It's unlikely that Kyto could have escaped," the queen said. "The chain was the strongest we could make. Still, we cannot be too careful. I'll send out a scout. In the meantime, don't say a word to anyone about this until we know more. I don't want to cause any panic. Understood?"

Silvermist and Fawn nodded. "Yes, Queen Clarion," they both said.

Chapter 5

Later that day, Silvermist hovered in the doorway of the kitchen, between the roots of the Home Tree. Inside, cooking-talent fairies were preparing the evening meal. A cauldron of fiddlehead stew simmered in the hearth. Wheels of cheese and loaves of crusty bread had been set aside, ready to be piled on serving trays. A row of chestnuts roasting on a spit gave off a wonderful smell. A sparrow man carefully turned them, making sure they browned evenly.

It was strange how normal everything seemed, Silvermist thought, when somewhere out there Kyto might be on the loose. She dabbed her damp brow with a petal kerchief. If there was one room in the Home Tree that made her uncomfortable, it was the kitchen. Too many fires. Unfortunately, she was stuck. She filled a thimble bucket from a nearby rain barrel, then went to stand again by the door.

Dulcie the baking-talent fairy was showing Necia around. "Cups go here, barrels of butter go there," Dulcie said. She marched through the kitchen, pointing out baskets full of rose-petal napkins, cabinets full of seashell plates, and rows of open shelves piled high with pots and pans. Necia was doing her best to keep up. But it was clear to Silvermist that the fire fairy wasn't pleased.

"Since Queen Clarion wants you to help, it will be your job to light the kitchen fires," Dulcie continued. "Oh, and you'll need one of these." She tossed Necia an apron.

Necia unfolded it and made a face. When she looked up, her eyes met Silvermist's.

Silvermist gave her a wry little smile. She'd meant it to be friendly. She knew how bossy Dulcie could be in the kitchen. But Necia scowled and looked away.

Does she know why I'm here? Silvermist wondered. *Did Queen Clarion tell her?*

"What time do we get started?" Necia asked, turning back to Dulcie.

Dulcie looked at Necia like she'd asked the most obvious question in the world. "At dawn, of course. I've got rolls and scones and cakes to make, all before breakfast."

"But that's so early!" Necia whined.

Dulcie leveled her eyes at Necia. "All the fairies in Pixie Hollow have a job to do."

"But *I'm* not a cooking talent," Necia said. "I'm a *fire* talent. Remember?"

Dulcie sighed. "Then let's put that talent of yours to use. The fire under those chestnut roasts needs to be stoked. See how it's gone down?"

Dulcie reached for some twigs to add to the fire. But Necia beat her to it. With a wave of her hand, the fire under the chestnuts flared up in a whoosh of roaring flames.

The sparrow man who had been turning them sprang back with a cry.

"My roasts!" Dulcie wailed.

The chestnuts were now blackened cinders. Dulcie threw up her hands in exasperation. "Necia, I said *stoke* the fire. Not incinerate our dinner!"

"I just thought they would cook faster if the flames were bigger," Necia said. "I'd fly backward."

But Silvermist noticed the sly smile twitching at the corners of the fire fairy's mouth. She had a feeling Necia wasn't sorry at all. In fact, she was sure that Necia had burned the roasts on purpose.

After the fire by the mill, things in Pixie Hollow had returned to normal, more or less. The fairies had gone back to picking fruit and measuring dust and making flowers bloom. And yet, Kate thought as she sat with her friends in the meadow, there was a feeling of tension in the air. It was as if the fire had cast a shadow over everything.

Her friends noticed it, too. "Maybe we should go home," Lainey suggested. "We can come back for another visit tomorrow."

"No!" Kate blurted. It came out louder than she'd meant. But Kate was sure they couldn't wait until tomorrow. Fawn had already gone to Queen Clarion with news of the dragon tracks. Who knew what steps the queen would take? By tomorrow, their chance could be gone.

"I *mean*, I've got a better idea," she added, lowering her voice. "I want to get a look at that dragon."

She'd barely gotten the words out before Mia was shaking her head. "Oh no, Kate. No way. You heard what Fawn said about Kyto. It's too dangerous."

"We'll be careful. We'll take fairy dust so we can fly away fast. And we won't get too close," Kate replied. "I've thought it all out. We won't do anything too risky."

"We don't even know where the dragon is," Lainey pointed out.

"We'll look for the rock at Torth Mountain where he was chained," Kate said. "If he's there, well, he'll be chained up, so we know it's safe. And if he isn't—no harm done."

"And what if we meet him on the way?" Mia asked.

"If Kyto really is loose, we won't be any safer in Pixie Hollow," Kate replied. "At least, if what Fawn says is true."

There was a moment of silence. "Come on," Kate said. "This is the only chance we'll ever have to see a real dragon. Aren't you even a little bit curious?"

"I'll go," Lainey said. "I guess I *am* sort of curious. It's a *dragon*, after all!"

"Excellent!" Kate beamed. "Mia?"

Mia pressed her lips into a tight line and cut her eyes at Gabby. Kate knew what she was trying to say. *We can't take Gabby to look for a dragon. She's too little!*

"What?" Gabby said loudly. "Why are you

looking at me like that? I want to go. I'm not afraid of any old dragon."

Kate grinned and folded her arms. "Well, Mia?"

"Oh, all right," Mia said with a sigh. "I'll go, only because I don't want Gabby to go without me. But I mean it, Kate. We're not taking any chances. The second we catch even a glimpse of the dragon, we're out of there."

"No problem," Kate said. "We won't stay long. I promise."

Chapter 6

Kate leaped off a rock and landed in the high grass of the meadow. Then she did a forward somersault, came up on one knee, and drew her pretend sword. "Take that, dragon!"

Lainey and Gabby, flying a few feet above Kate's head, laughed out loud. Mia, bringing up the rear, made a face and landed next to Kate.

"Shouldn't we be there by now?" Mia asked. "It feels like we've been flying for hours."

When they'd started out from Pixie Hollow, Torth Mountain hadn't looked that far away. They could see it looming in the distance, the tallest peak in Never Land. But though the mountain seemed to get bigger as they flew toward it, it never seemed to get closer.

"Wait," Lainey said, cocking her head. "What's that sound?"

Kate stood still and listened. There *was* a sound, like leaves blowing in the breeze or . . . water! "It must be the Wough River!"

Kate took a running start, pushed off the ground, and sailed into the air. Her friends followed. After a few minutes of flying, they came over a rise. Below them, a wide, rushing river stretched for miles. Not far beyond it were jagged cliffs and the rocky base of Torth Mountain.

"We're almost there!" she cried.

Mia, Lainey, and Gabby followed Kate's finger with their eyes. Torth Mountain stretched high into the sky. Near the top, it narrowed to a snowy peak.

"The mountain is huge!" Mia said. "Kyto's

rock could be anywhere."

"Fawn said Kyto was chained to a rock at the *base* of the mountain," Kate said. "So that's where we should start looking."

As they continued flying, Kate noticed that the ground below her changed from soft, high grasses to sandy pebbles, then to terra-cotta-colored clay and large boulders.

Soon they could fly no farther. A vertical wall of rock stood before them.

Kate floated gently to the ground. "I guess we've reached the base?"

Gabby and Lainey nodded. They didn't seem as enthusiastic as they had before. Mia pushed her hair out of her eyes and looked around nervously.

"All right, Kyto," Kate murmured anxiously to herself. "Where are you hiding?"

As they continued on foot, the sky began to darken. She looked up and saw that a cloud had drifted in front of the sun. A chilly breeze suddenly whipped past her. She shivered and covered her arms.

"Maybe we should turn back," Mia said.

"But we've come all this way!" Kate replied. "We can't give up now."

They walked on, weaving between scattered boulders. As they walked, Kate gradually became aware of a foul odor.

Lainey stopped and wrinkled her nose. "What's that smell?"

Gabby and Mia covered their noses, too. "It stinks like rotten eggs!" Mia said.

A sound made them jump. It was a slow hissing, like steam releasing from a valve. Kate's heart thudded. *Could it be . . . ?*

Putting her finger to her lips, Kate motioned her friends forward. Ahead was a rocky outcropping. The girls crept toward it. As quietly as they could, they scrambled up the steep rocks.

Mia was the first to reach the top. She gasped, then clapped a hand over her mouth. Kate came up next and peered down. What she saw made her skin break out in prickles.

Below them, the dragon was stretched out on the ground. His body, covered in blue-green scales, was nearly as big as an elephant's, but his long neck and tail made him seem much bigger. His veiny purple wings were folded across his back. He had a narrow, bony head and cruel eyes. A puff of white smoke issued from each nostril.

Kate gagged and her eyes watered—the awful smell was coming from him.

The dragon shifted slightly, and Kate heard the clink of metal. She spotted the thick silver chain fastened to a collar around his neck. The opposite end had been driven into a giant boulder.

Then she heard another sound—a slow scraping, like a knife being sharpened. Kyto

was raking his talons against a rock, drumming them like fingers. The sound made Kate's hair stand on end.

Kyto was nothing like what she'd imagined. He was no fairy-tale dragon. He was horrifyingly real.

A sharp tug on Kate's shirt made her jump. She whirled around, but it was only Gabby.

"I don't like this," Gabby whispered. "Can we go?" She looked as frightened as Kate felt.

Kate nodded. For once, she'd had all the adventure she needed.

But as she turned to leave, a glimmer of light caught her eye. Kate paused. She had been so distracted by the dragon's terrible appearance, she hadn't noticed the pile of gold coins at his feet. Looking closer, she noticed the neat piles of strange and precious things—an ornate silver cup, rubies, ropes of pearls, books with moldering leather covers, marble statues, strangely colored feathers, and things Kate couldn't even begin to identify.

"Kyto's treasure hoard!" she whispered under her breath.

She leaned forward for a better view. As she did, a small pebble dislodged from beneath her hand. It went bouncing down the side of the rocks and rolled to a stop only inches away from the dragon.

Kate froze in horror.

Kyto's head slithered up from the ground. In a voice like a nest of snakes, he rasped, "Come out, you."

Kate glanced at her friends, who looked

just as petrified. What should they do? Kate wasn't sure they could make a run for it. Her knees seemed to have gone weak.

At that moment, she heard the flutter of wings. Another voice, this one high and bell-like, said, "Kyto."

Kate peeked around the rock again. Two fairies were hovering above the dragon, just out of his reach. She recognized them right away—Myka, a scout talent, and Spring, a messenger. What were they doing?

The fairies didn't seem to have noticed Kate and her friends. They were looking right at Kyto. Kate signaled to her friends to be quiet. She had a feeling the fairies wouldn't like them being there.

When Kyto saw the fairies, his eyes narrowed. "Ah, two preciousss fairies from Pixie

Hollow. To what do I owe the pleasssure?" As he spoke, a little trail of white smoke escaped his lips.

"Queen Clarion sent us," Myka said.

"To sssend her regardsss?" There was a rumble like distant thunder as Kyto chuckled at his own joke. "No, I sssuppossse not."

"We thought you might have . . ." Spring trailed off.

"Essscaped?" Kyto said, finishing her sentence. "No. I'm ssstill here, as you can sssee." He tapped the long silver chain lying in the dirt.

Myka nodded. Then she turned to Spring and said something in a low voice. Kate caught the word *tracks*.

So that's it, she thought. *Fawn told Queen Clarion about the tracks. The queen must have sent them to make sure Kyto was still chained up.*

And he was. Fawn had been wrong about the dragon tracks after all.

Kyto was watching the fairies through slitted eyes. Even though they were talking quietly, Kate had the sense he was listening to every word.

"Ssso you've ssseen her," the dragon hissed suddenly. "And now you've come to me for help."

The fairies looked at him. "What do you mean?" Spring asked sharply. "Seen who?"

Kyto took a step toward her. "The new dragon."

Kate looked at her friends and mouthed the words *A new dragon?* Mia's and Lainey's eyes grew wide. Gabby covered her mouth with her hands.

"Yesss, another dragon," Kyto repeated.

He took two more steps closer to the fairies. He was straining at the end of his chain now. "I've driven her away once, but she'll come back. She'sss after my hoard. I can't fight her off, chained up like thisss. But if you let me go, I could crissssp her!"

There was something in Kyto's slithery voice that Kate didn't trust. *It's a trick!* she silently yelled to the fairies. *Don't listen to him!* The idea of Kyto on the loose made her break into a cold sweat.

Spring and Myka seemed unimpressed, however. "A new dragon on Never Land?" Myka asked. "Strange that this is the first we've heard of it."

Spring regarded Kyto. "I think you'd say anything to get us to undo the chain."

Kyto suddenly lunged at them, snapping

his needle-like teeth. *"Release me!"* he roared. Spring and Myka darted back, barely dodging the stream of fire that shot from his mouth.

Kyto flapped his wings, rising a few feet off the ground. He let out a horrible, screeching roar and shot another flame in their direction.

"Flame all you want, Kyto," Spring called. "We won't set you free."

The fight seemed to go out of Kyto. He turned and crept heavily back to his shiny piles, curling himself around them. "Then go away and leave me alone!" he snarled.

The girls heard a whir of wings. Myka and Spring were gone without saying goodbye. Kate was ready to go, too. Together the girls began climbing down from the rock.

Kate had just reached the bottom, when she heard Kyto's voice again, softer this time.

"Don't worry," he whispered. "I'll protect you."

Who was he talking to? Kate peeked around the rocks. Kyto was nosing among the items in his hoard, murmuring. He was talking to his treasure!

"*Pssst.* Kate! Let's go!" Lainey whispered behind her. Mia and Gabby were already moving away.

At that moment, Kyto looked up. His eyes locked onto Kate's.

With a gasp, Kate sprang away from the rock and raced after her friends.

For a long time, no one said anything. Kate's insides felt like jelly, as if Kyto had looked right through her and turned them to mush. They had reached the Wough River by the time she found her voice again.

"Well, that was fun." She laughed nervously.

"Yeah, a real treat," Mia said.

"But what are they going to do about the new dragon?" Gabby whispered. "Will the fairies catch that one, too?"

"There isn't another dragon," Kate said. She gave Gabby a comforting squeeze. "Kyto was playing a trick."

"How do you know for sure?" Lainey asked.

"You heard Spring. Kyto would say anything to get free." Kate thought of the dragon's awful eyes, and the shrewd way he'd watched the fairies. "He just *looks* like a liar."

"But what about the tracks we found?"

Mia asked.

"We don't know for sure they were dragon tracks," Kate pointed out. "Fawn never saw them. She jumped to a conclusion."

Lainey's forehead furrowed. "That doesn't sound like Fawn."

"I'm glad there's no more dragons," Gabby said. "I don't want to see another dragon ever again."

"Me neither," Kate said. She reached into her pocket for more fairy dust. "Come on. Let's go home."

Chapter 7

"Unchain me!" Kyto roared.

Kate ran as fast as her legs would carry her, but she could feel the heat from the dragon's breath on her back. She could smell his awful stench. With every step, he was gaining on her. Any second, he would reach out and—

"Ahhh!" Kate sat up in her bed with a start.

Daylight was streaming through the window blinds. Her soccer ball sat in the corner. Yesterday's clothes were tossed over the back of her chair. She breathed a sigh of relief. She was in her own bed, in her own room, at home.

It was only a dream, she told herself.

Kate threw off her quilt and climbed out of bed. She put on yesterday's jeans and a clean T-shirt, shoved her feet into her slippers, and went downstairs.

In the kitchen, her mother was standing at the counter with a cup of coffee in one hand and a half-eaten piece of toast in the other. She was dressed in nice pants and a sweater.

"Oh, good. You're up," she said when Kate sat down at the table. "I have a volunteer meeting this morning." Her mom was on a bunch of different committees. Kate could never keep track of them all.

Kate's mother took a closer look at her. "Are you feeling okay?"

"Yes," Kate mumbled. The feeling of the Kyto dream still clung to her. She gave a little shiver, as if to shake it off, and reached for a carton of juice. "I'm fine. I'll probably go over to Mia's house after breakfast."

On Saturdays, Kate and her friends

usually spent the whole day in Never Land. But today she was in no hurry to get there. The image of Kyto lingered in her mind.

Her mom nodded. "That's fine. Dad's out running errands. He'll be home soon, but leave a note if you go to Mia's before he gets back, okay?"

Kate nodded. Her mother kissed the top of her head and headed out the door.

Kate poured herself a bowl of cereal, then went to the front door to look for the newspaper. She hoped reading the comics would make her forget about dragons for a while.

As she took the paper off the stoop, she noticed the Johnsons' house. The porch swing was gone. So were the curtains in the windows. The house had a blank, empty look. The only colorful things that remained were the flowering azalea bush—and the big SOLD sign on the front lawn.

Kate stared at the bright pink flowers. How many times had she seen Mr. Johnson watering them with the garden hose? Or Mrs. Johnson snipping blossoms to put in a vase? It seemed as much a part of the couple as their smiles.

Suddenly, Kate felt furious. She didn't like the idea of strangers living in the Johnsons' house. It didn't seem right that people who didn't even *know* the Johnsons should get to enjoy those flowers.

Setting down the paper, Kate marched across the street. She stopped in front of the azalea bush. It was in full bloom, each flower a brilliant burst of color next to the empty house.

Kate picked up a stick and began to whack at the flowers, sending the petals flying. She kept at it until she was breathing hard. When she was done, the ground looked like it was covered with pink confetti.

Looking at the ruined bush, Kate felt a strange satisfaction. *Serves them right for making the Johnsons move,* she thought.

As she crossed the street, she tossed the stick away. Then she picked up the newspaper and went back into her house.

That same morning, in Pixie Hollow, Silvermist was ready for a break from the kitchen. She'd been up since dawn watching Necia light fires and squabble with the cooking fairies. As the cleaning fairies cleared up from the morning meal, she slipped into the tearoom.

The room was almost empty. Soft light filtered through the tall sea-grass curtains. Silvermist poured herself a cup of blackberry tea and sighed. It was nice to be somewhere calm after the heat and clamor of the kitchen.

Across the room, she saw Tinker Bell, Rosetta, and a caterpillar shearer named Nettle lingering over their own cups of tea. She fluttered over to join them.

"He thought we'd *unchain* him," Tink was saying, shaking her head. "As if we'd be fooled so easily."

"You can't trust anything Kyto says," Rosetta agreed.

Somehow word had gotten out about

Spring and Myka's visit to Kyto. It had been the talk of Pixie Hollow ever since they returned.

Nettle dunked a poppy puff into her tea. "Well," she said between bites, "what if it was true? What if there *was* another dragon?"

"What a horrible thought!" Rosetta said.

"Don't be silly, Nettle," Tink replied. "The scouts would have spotted it by—"

CRASH!

The sounds of pots and pans clattering to the floor echoed through the tearoom. A moment later, the door to the kitchen swung open. Necia, soaking wet from head to toe, stomped across the room, leaving a trail of watery footprints behind her.

Silvermist and the other fairies stared. Necia glared back at them. Then she lifted

her chin and marched through the door that led outside.

"She's got quite a fiery temper, doesn't she?" Nettle remarked when she was gone. "Guess Dulcie must have tried to cool her off with a pot of water."

"I heard she burned Dulcie's chestnut roasts to a crisp," Rosetta said.

"I heard she torched a whole batch of tea cakes," Tink added. "Is it true, Silvermist?"

Silvermist nodded unhappily. Necia's time in the kitchen had been one cooking disaster after another. "I can't imagine why Queen Clarion thought she'd be any help." She finished the last of her tea and stood up with a sigh. "I guess this means my break is over," she said, starting for the door.

"Good luck," Tink called after her.

Silvermist walked slowly to the door, dragging her feet a little. She wished she could have at least a few more moments of quiet before chasing after Necia.

In the bright sunlight, she shaded her eyes and looked for the fire fairy. But Necia wasn't in the courtyard.

Silvermist circled the Home Tree, but there was no sign of her. Could she have gone to her room? Silvermist wondered. But why hadn't she passed her on the way in?

Silvermist went once around the Home Tree again. Then she flew in wider and wider circles, looking everywhere.

The fire fairy was gone.

Chapter 8

Later that day, in Never Land, Kate waved good-bye to her friends and set off alone into the forest. Lainey had plans to help the butterfly herders that day, and Mia and Gabby were collecting strawberries with the harvest fairies. But Kate was determined to get another look at those animal tracks. *If Kyto didn't make them,* she wondered, *what did?*

She followed a deer trail in the direction she remembered. When the trail ended, she pushed on, making her way slowly through the tangles of trees and vines.

Before long, she came across the charred remains of a tree. The bushes around it had burned as well. But was it the same place they'd been before? The burned area looked bigger than Kate remembered. And there hadn't been a tree before, had there? Could there have been *another* small forest fire?

Kate walked toward where she remembered seeing the tracks, scanning the ground carefully. At the edge of the burned area, she found an indentation in the soft dirt. It might have been a print of some sort. But it was hard to say for sure.

She stepped backward, searching for more. *CRUNCH!*

Kate looked down and saw that she'd stepped on something brittle and dry. As she bent to get a better look, she felt a sharp sting.

Ouch! She slapped at her forearm. A little red welt was forming on her arm. She heard buzzing.

That was a bee's nest! Kate realized, just as a cloud of bees rose around her.

Run! Kate took off at a sprint. She frantically smacked at her arms and face, but she felt another sting, and another. Kate vaulted over a log. She splashed across a brook. She trampled through leaves and swatted away tree branches. But no matter how fast she ran, she couldn't outrun the swarm.

Kate pumped her legs, running faster and faster . . . until suddenly she was running through a fog of thick white smoke.

Kate coughed and slowed. She spun around, expecting to see the forest in flames.

Instead, she saw Necia! The fire fairy was hovering above a nearby palm tree. One of the fronds was smoldering. Necia fanned her wings, sending plumes of white smoke wafting toward the bees.

As the smoke hit them, the bees slowed and seemed to grow confused. The swarm began to quiet down.

Kate looked on in awe. "You're a bee charmer!" she gasped when she finally managed to catch her breath.

"Not really." Necia fanned her wings a few more times. "It's the smoke. I'm not sure why, but it calms bees down."

The bees flew in sleepy circles, ignoring Kate and the fairy. When it seemed safe, Necia left the palm branch and flew over to Kate. "Are you all right?"

"I think so." Kate's arm was throbbing. She shakily counted up the bee stings. Aside from the one on her arm, she had two on her right hand, and one more on the back of her neck. But Kate knew it could have been much, much worse.

"You saved me!" Kate had an urge to reach out and hug the fairy.

Necia's glow brightened. "I'm glad I could," she said.

"But . . . what are you doing out here all by yourself?" Kate asked.

At once, Necia's face closed off. "Nothing. I just want to be alone."

"It's all right," Kate said, sensing a secret. "I won't tell."

Necia hesitated. She looked around as if to make sure that she and Kate were truly alone. "Promise?"

Kate nodded.

"I'm practicing," Necia whispered.

"Practicing what?" Kate asked.

"Watch." Necia snapped her fingers, and once again a spark appeared. With her breath and hands, she coaxed the spark into flame.

Kate looked on in awe. The fire sat right in Necia's cupped hands, but the fairy didn't seem to feel any pain. She raised one hand, as if pulling a needle through cloth. The flames followed.

As Necia pushed and pulled, the flames took shape. A head appeared, then a beak, then a pair of wings. She flung her hands upward, and the fire-hawk flew into the air. It hung there for a moment, blazing against the blue sky.

Necia called up another flame and formed it in the shape of a rabbit. With a wave of her hand, the fire-rabbit went hopping through the trees. The fire-hawk soared after it, then swooped. The moment they touched, both vanished.

"Wow!" Kate whispered. "Can you make *anything* out of fire?"

In answer, Necia snapped her fingers again. In moments, a fire-fairy was hovering in the air. The flames of her wings flickered as if they were fluttering. The curl of fire then made her head bob. She looked like she was nodding.

Kate clapped her hands with delight. "Have you shown the other fairies?"

"No."

"Why not? It's amazing!"

Necia waved her hands, and the fairy dissolved into the air. "Queen Clarion says I'm not supposed to be making fires without *supervision*." She made a face. "I sneak into the forest whenever I can to practice. Queen Clarion would be upset if she knew I was here. She wants me to spend all day lighting cooking fires."

"But you can do so much more than that!" Kate said.

"The other fairies don't think so. And you can't tell them! They don't understand my talent." Necia paused and looked down. "I think they're all afraid of me."

Kate remembered the horrified looks on the other fairies' faces the day of Necia's arrival. She didn't know what to say. After all, she hadn't understood how amazing Necia's fire talent could be, either.

"Sometimes I think my laugh must have gotten lost," Necia went on. Her voice was so quiet Kate had to strain to hear her. "Maybe I was supposed to arrive somewhere else, someplace where there are other fairies like me. It's hard not having any friends."

Kate was stunned. Necia seemed so strong

and confident and powerful. It had never occurred to Kate how lonely she might be.

"*I'll* be your friend," Kate said.

Necia looked up. "Because I saved you from the bees?"

"Because you saved me from the bees. And also because you're nice and fun and your talent is the coolest of all the fairy talents."

"Do you really think so?"

"Of course! And Mia and Lainey and Gabby will be your friends, too. I know they'll like you."

Necia's glow had gradually grown brighter. Now she shone like a hot coal. "In that case, friend, should we go back to Pixie Hollow? I'd love to meet them all. Maybe we can have the midday meal together. It would be nice to have friends to eat with for once."

The change in Necia was remarkable. Her sullen expression was gone. She seemed to be bubbling over with excitement. *She just needed someone to be friendly to her,* Kate thought. "Actually, I'm hungry, too," she told the fairy. "Let's go."

Kate and Necia headed back in the direction of Pixie Hollow, around the thickets and streams, chatting and laughing the whole way. But when they reached the edge of the woods, Necia stopped and turned to her.

"Please don't tell anyone what I showed you. And don't tell them I was practicing my talent in the woods," she said. "I've had enough trouble as it is."

Kate tapped her shoulder, indicating for Necia to catch a ride. "Your secret is safe with me."

Chapter 9

Silvermist hovered in the orchard. She looked around at the burned grass and the scorched tree trunks and shook her head. Another fire had broken out in the forest, and this one had spread all the way to the fairies' orchard.

Luckily, the water fairies had been able to get the flames under control before they got out of hand. They had only lost two peach trees and a large patch of marigolds. But Silvermist was furious. She was sure the fire was Necia's fault.

That fiery temper! Had she set the blaze on purpose? Silvermist wondered. Just like she'd burned Dulcie's chestnut roasts?

And I was supposed to be keeping an eye on her! Silvermist put her head in her hands. She knew Necia had deliberately given her the slip. And now Silvermist would have to take the blame for letting the new fairy out of her sight.

"You look tired," Rani said, putting a hand on Silvermist's shoulder. "The other water fairies and I can finish here. Why don't you go get some rest?"

Silvermist *was* exhausted. "Are you sure?"

Rani nodded. "You've had a rough few days, with all the firefighting and the fairy-sitting. You should take a break."

Silvermist thanked Rani and started for her room in the Home Tree. But as she flew, she couldn't calm down. Her mind kept going back to that morning, when she had lingered in the tearoom.

If only I had followed Necia instead of sitting with the other fairies, maybe I could have prevented another fire, she chastised herself. Queen Clarion would no doubt be livid.

The realization stopped Silvermist in midair. *I should go back.* If the queen found out she'd gone off for a nap and left the work to the other water fairies, what would she think? At the same time, Silvermist was in no rush to get back to the fire.

As Silvermist hovered there, she saw Kate emerging from the woods. And who was riding atop her shoulder but Necia! Kate and the fire fairy were laughing over some shared joke. In fact, Silvermist noted angrily, it looked like they were having a grand time.

The nerve! Silvermist fumed. How could Necia be laughing and having fun when so many fairies were cleaning up after another one of her fires?

Silvermist started toward them, getting madder by the second. She stopped right in front of Kate's nose, exclaiming, "Necia! Where have you been?"

Kate drew up short, and Necia nearly tumbled off her shoulder. "What do you mean?" Necia asked when she'd caught her balance.

Silvermist folded her arms. Her foot tapped furiously in the air. "How could you start another fire and fly away without telling anyone? All of Never Land could have burned!"

Necia stole a quick glance at Kate. "I don't know what you're talking about," she said.

"The fire in the orchard, Necia. Just now.

If some water fairies hadn't been close by—"

Necia fluttered forward. "The orchard? Silvermist, I honestly don't know what you're talking about."

As the argument continued, more and more fairies came out from the Home Tree and the surrounding bushes to gawk.

Silvermist put her hands on her hips and rolled her eyes. "So you're claiming you *didn't* start that fire?"

"Yes," Necia snapped through clenched teeth. "That's exactly what I'm saying. Are you calling me a liar?"

"Enough! Everyone calm down."

Silvermist dropped her hands from her hips as Queen Clarion flew through the crowd. She couldn't remember the last time

Pixie Hollow had been so quiet. Even the birds had stopped chirping, and the breeze had gone still.

"Now," the queen said, taking a deep breath, "someone explain to me what is going on."

"Necia started another fire in the orchard, and she pretends to know nothing about it!" Silvermist exclaimed.

"I did not!" Necia cried.

The queen held up her hand to silence them. "Silvermist, did you see this happen?"

"No," Silvermist admitted.

The queen raised her eyebrows. "But you were with Necia, weren't you?"

"I don't need anyone to *watch* me," Necia interjected.

The queen held up her hand again.

Instantly, Necia closed her mouth.

"Silvermist?"

"I *was* with Necia in the kitchen, Queen Clarion," Silvermist said, wishing she could disappear into the ground. "But then she left, and when I went looking for her, I couldn't find her. I'd fly backward."

The queen sighed. "All right. Necia, can you tell me what you've been doing since then?"

Silvermist watched as Necia fiddled with her dress. "Nothing."

"Nothing?" the queen said. "*Where* were you doing nothing?"

Necia was silent.

"Necia, if you can't tell me where you've been or what you've been doing, I'll assume that you're not being truthful."

The queen waited for a response, but Necia only looked away.

Queen Clarion sighed and shook her head. "Then you've given me no choice. You are hereby forbidden from making fires ever again."

The crowd erupted in gasps. A fairy's talent was her greatest joy! This was serious punishment indeed.

"Excuse me, Queen Clarion?"

To Silvermist's surprise, Kate was stepping forward. "I . . . I really don't think this fire was Necia's fault," Kate said.

Another round of murmurs broke out. Why was *Kate* getting involved? Silvermist wondered.

"Why is that, Kate?" the queen asked.

Kate glanced at Necia. The fire fairy

frowned and gave a slight shake of her head. "Um . . . it's just . . . ," Kate stammered. "I . . . don't think she did it."

"I appreciate your opinion," the queen replied. "But if Necia can't tell me where she's been, or how the fire in the orchard started, I have no choice but to suspend her talent. I've made up my mind."

A gasp burst from Necia, and she darted away toward the Home Tree. The crowd began to break up.

Silvermist watched, feeling confused. She should have been pleased. Necia had broken the rules and gotten what she deserved. But instead she felt even more troubled.

There had been tears in Necia's eyes. It surprised Silvermist that the fire fairy who hated water so much was crying.

Chapter 10

Kate looked up at the sky, which was turning gold, orange, purple, and blue. The sun was setting behind Torth Mountain. She wrapped her arms around herself and shivered. It was almost always warm in Never Land, but the air had grown chilly. A gust of wind whipped through the tall grasses and shook the trees. She headed toward the hollow tree that held the portal back to their world, feeling terrible.

"Kate," Mia said, "why were you sticking up for Necia back there?"

Kate shook her head and kicked a pinecone. It tumbled end over end before slamming into the tree trunk. "I can't tell you."

Mia's forehead furrowed. "Why not?"

"I promised Necia I wouldn't say. But now I don't know what to do," Kate said.

"You can tell us, Kate. We're your friends," Lainey said.

Kate looked from one to the other. They *were* her friends, and she knew they would understand. Maybe they could even help.

Necia had trusted her with her secret. But it was clear to Kate that she needed help.

Was it okay to break her promise if it might actually do some good?

Kate decided to risk it. Taking a deep breath, she told her friends about meeting Necia in the forest. She explained how Necia had saved her from the bees and shown Kate her amazing talent. "That's how I know she didn't start the fire in the orchard," Kate said. "She couldn't have, because she was in the woods with me."

"But why didn't you say all that?" Lainey asked. "Just tell Queen Clarion what happened. Then she'll let Necia do her magic again."

"I wanted to," Kate said. "But I was afraid I'd get Necia in even more trouble. She was already breaking the rules. She wasn't supposed to be making fire on her own, especially not in the woods."

"It's the orchard fire everyone's upset about," Mia said. "Why wouldn't Necia want to tell everyone what she was doing if it could prove the fire wasn't her fault?"

Kate had been puzzled about that, too. "I think," she said slowly, working it out in her mind, "I think maybe she's afraid. She thinks the other fairies are already scared of her. If they see what she can really do, maybe things will be even worse."

"It's not fair," Gabby said. "The queen took away her talent and she didn't do anything wrong."

"It's *not* fair," Kate agreed. "But it's up to Necia whether she wants to share her talent with other fairies."

"I still think we should tell," Mia said. "Necia shouldn't have to take the blame for something that isn't her fault."

"What if we did, and we only got Necia into more trouble?" Kate pointed out, looking from Mia to Lainey to Gabby. "Tomorrow we'll go to the orchard and look for clues to what started that fire. Maybe we can find a way to prove she's innocent. Until then, we can't say anything. Do you guys promise?"

Mia sighed. "Okay, I promise."

"Me too," Lainey said.

"Promise." Gabby pretended to twist a key over her lips and toss the key away.

Kate stepped inside the hollow tree and began feeling her way through the dark. For the first time ever, she was actually looking forward to going home.

The following afternoon, Kate, Mia, Gabby, and Lainey sat in Kate's living room, finishing their home-work. Kate was supposed to be writing a report on pioneers, but she couldn't get past the

first sentence. It was hard to think about settlers and covered wagons when her mind was stuck in Never Land. She couldn't stop thinking about Necia. If the fire fairy hadn't caused the blaze in the orchard, what had?

At last, she threw down her pencil and stood up. "I need a break. Who wants lemonade?"

"Me," said Lainey, without looking up from her worksheet.

"Me too," said Mia. Her pencil darted across the page as she worked on her report.

"And me," said Gabby as she finished a math problem.

Kate watched them enviously. Their homework would be done before hers was even started. If only there were a wand she could wave to finish it.

As she started for the kitchen, something outside the window caught her eye. There were people in the Johnsons' house! A woman sat on the front porch, holding a baby in her lap. The woman was blowing bubbles with a little wand. Every time she blew another bunch of bubbles, the baby laughed and tried to catch them in her plump fist.

Kate stared. When had they moved in? How could she not have noticed?

Kate wanted to dislike the new family, she really did. It was their fault that the Johnsons had moved away. But watching the mother and baby laughing together, she had to admit they seemed sort of . . . nice.

Kate thought of the ruined azalea, and shame suddenly washed over her.

"What are you looking at?" Mia asked, glancing up from her paper.

"Nothing." Kate turned away from the window, but Mia got up to look anyway.

"Oh!" she exclaimed. "You have new neighbors. Have you met them yet?"

"No, Mia," Kate snapped. "I've had way more important things to think about, like Necia and Kyto and finishing this dumb report about pioneers. Okay?"

Mia looked taken aback. "Okay. Sorry."

"Who cares about the new neighbors anyway?" Kate grumbled. With a huff, she stomped off to the kitchen in search of the lemonade.

Chapter 11

Silvermist sat at the edge of Havendish Stream, dreamily watching the water flow past. Now that Necia had been forbidden to make fires, Silvermist no longer had to keep an eye on her. She could finally hang out again with the other water fairies.

"It's good to be back to normal," she said to Rani, who was sitting with her. She waved to a group of other water fairies sailing past in their leaf-boats. They waved back and called to her to join them.

"Want to?" asked Rani.

"Yes!" Silvermist hadn't been out sailing since the day of Necia's arrival. How nice it would be to get back on the water!

As she stood, she noticed Kate, Mia, Lainey, and Gabby in the orchard on the opposite bank. They were poking around the burned trees as if they were looking for something.

"What are they doing?" Rani asked.

"I don't know," Silvermist replied. "Did you notice how Kate jumped to defend Necia yesterday?"

"I did," Rani said. "It was strange."

"She sounded so certain," Silvermist said.

"Do you suppose Necia somehow talked Kate into taking her side? And why would Kate go along with her?"

"Who knows? We'll never understand the ways of Clumsies," Rani said with a shrug. "Come on."

Together they made their way to the dock where the sailboats were tied. Silvermist's was a fine skiff made of birch bark with a red sea-grape leaf for a sail. She had designed it herself with help from a shipbuilding fairy.

Silvermist began to undo the knot. "We should talk to the carpenter fairies about making a new boat launch. Don't you think? . . . Rani, what's wrong?"

Rani was looking up at the sky. She sniffed the air, frowning. "Do you smell that?"

The wind shifted, and then Silvermist

smelled it, too. "Oh no! It couldn't be."

She looked over her shoulder. In the distance, beyond the meadow and the fairy circle, she saw clouds of black smoke rising from the trees.

Rani gasped. "Another fire!"

"But the queen forbid her to make fires!" Silvermist wailed.

"You think Necia caused it?" Rani asked.

"Who else?" Silvermist couldn't believe the fire fairy had done this again. She didn't think she had the energy to fight another fire. "You call in the water fairies. I'll fly to the Home Tree and send out a warning. Hopefully, it's not too close to Pixie Hollow this time." Silvermist started for the Home Tree at top speed.

But as she got close, she stopped short in surprise. Necia was sitting alone in the courtyard. The fire fairy's chin was cupped in her hand. She stared into space with a dull expression.

"But if she's here . . . ," Silvermist murmured. Was it possible this fire wasn't Necia's fault after all?

Other fairies had spotted the smoke, too. They came flying in from the meadow. A few were fluttering out of their rooms in the Home Tree. Kate and the other girls came running up from the orchard.

"We smelled smoke!" Kate said.

"What's going on?" Tinker Bell asked as she and Prilla flew up to Silvermist.

"Another fire. Somewhere beyond the fairy circle," Silvermist replied.

"Where's Necia?" Tink asked.

Silvermist gestured to the courtyard. "She's there. I . . . I actually don't think she could have started this one."

She saw Kate glance at Mia and raise her eyebrows. Mia nodded ever so slightly. *What's that about?* Silvermist wondered. She had the feeling they knew something she didn't.

But there wasn't time to think about it now. "Are the other water fairies on their way to help?" Tink was asking.

Silvermist's attention snapped back to her. "Rani's gathering them now. We need to know how big the fire is. Prilla, can you find one of the scouts? . . . Prilla?"

Prilla was looking past them up at the sky. Her mouth hung open in astonishment.

"Look!" Gabby squealed.

Something was coming toward them through the sky. Its long neck undulated like a sea serpent as it flew. Its great wings cast a shadow over the forest as it passed.

"Is that what I think it is?" Mia whispered.

"Kyto wasn't lying!" Tink said with a gasp. "There *is* another dragon!"

With two flaps of its great wings, the

dragon reached Pixie Hollow. The fairies screamed and scattered. The dragon opened its jaws. A white-hot blast shot from the dragon's mouth, and the top of the Home Tree burst into flame.

Chapter 12

It was a scene from a nightmare. Panicked fairies spilled from the Home Tree as flames spread across the topmost branches. Silvermist looked around for something to help.

Her eyes fell on a nearby puddle. Darting down, she threw a pinch of fairy dust on it. Then she took the edge of the muddy water in her hands, as one might grasp a blanket, and pulled with all her might. The puddle peeled away from the ground with a loud sucking sound.

Silvermist struggled back up into the air, dragging it behind her. She beat her wings with all her might, but she couldn't fly fast enough. The muddy water was too heavy.

Other fairies moved out of her way, but they couldn't help. Only a water fairy could grasp water without spilling it.

"Marina!" Silvermist cried, spying another water fairy at last. "Help me!"

Marina flew over and took the other side of the puddle. Together they flew up and dropped it over the fire. A few branches sizzled. But the fire was still spreading.

"Silvermist! We're coming!" voices cried.

The other water fairies, summoned by

Rani, were flying in from the stream. They carried leaves filled with water. The fairies dipped their hands into the leaves and lobbed balls of water at the fire. Silvermist joined them, grabbing handfuls of water from their makeshift buckets.

"Look out below!" a voice cried.

Silvermist looked up and saw Fawn on the back of a pelican. She darted out of the way as the bird emptied a mouthful of water onto the fire.

"It's coming back!" someone screamed.

The dragon was turning around, its long body drawing a half circle in the air. It came toward them again, flying so low that the tip of its tail knocked leaves from the tops of trees.

As it came over Pixie Hollow, the fairies

all dove for cover again. But it didn't fire another blast. The dragon kept going, turning north toward Torth Mountain.

Silvermist watched it soar into the distance. *We're safe,* she thought. *But for how long?*

They kept fighting the fire, and slowly it began to die. When the last flames were extinguished, Silvermist and the other exhausted firefighters made their way to the fairy circle. The magical ring of toadstools was where they held their most important meetings.

Every fairy in Pixie Hollow had crowded into the circle. Some were crying. Others looked dazed. No one had been hurt in the fire, but more than a dozen fairies had lost their rooms in the Home Tree.

Queen Clarion moved through the crowd,

speaking gently to the fairies who were most upset. Silvermist knew soon she would call a meeting. But the queen's first instinct was to calm everyone down. She was a good ruler that way.

Silvermist saw some of her friends standing together. She pushed her way over to them, looking pale and tense. The fairies frantically discussed what to do.

"I knew something was wrong," Fawn was saying. "I was sure those tracks couldn't belong to anything but a dragon."

"Do you think we can trap this one like we trapped Kyto?" Rosetta asked.

"We'd have to make another chain, an even bigger one this time," Tink said. She sounded pleased at the idea. As a tinkering fairy, Tink loved to make things.

"Don't forget what it was like catching Kyto," Fawn warned. "This new dragon could be even more dangerous."

"Never fairies." Queen Clarion's bell-like voice rang out to the crowd. Everyone quieted to hear what she would say.

"Today has been terrible," the queen said. "But don't despair. We can overcome this as we have before."

"How?" someone cried out.

"Will we make another trap?" someone else exclaimed.

"What if we took Kyto's advice?" Prilla asked. "We could set him free and let him fight off the new dragon."

The crowd murmured in outrage. The idea was insane!

The queen held up her hands for quiet. "I have decided we will go to Kyto for help." This shocked the fairies into silence for a moment.

The crowd erupted in cries of outrage. Finally, Tink spoke up. "But, Queen Clarion," Tink said, raising her voice, "if we let him go, we might never be free of him again. . . . It's too dangerous. The last thing we need is *two* dragons on the loose."

"I didn't say let him go, Tink," the queen replied. "I said we'll go to him for help. He may be able to give us advice. If there's one creature on Never Land who might know how to defeat a dragon, it's Kyto."

The crowd broke into murmurs again.

"Why would Kyto help us?" someone shouted.

"How can we possibly trust a dragon?" said another voice.

The queen waited until they had quieted down. "I think there could be something we can do for him," she said. "We may be able to arrange a trade. If Kyto helps us defeat this new dragon, we'll offer to bring him a new item for his hoard. The most important thing in the world to a dragon is his treasure, after all."

"What kind of item?" Tink asked.

The queen shook her head and sighed. "We'll have to ask Kyto what he wants. But you can be sure that he'll ask for something extremely rare."

Silvermist knew the queen was right. But what could they possibly have that Kyto would want?

"Now, we'll need volunteers," the queen continued. "We have a lot of work to do."

Tinker Bell was the first to flutter forward. "I'll go."

Brave Tink, Silvermist thought. She could always be counted on.

Silvermist raised her hand. "I will, too." She didn't like the idea of visiting Kyto. But she knew her talent would be needed. The queen nodded, looking relieved.

"You'll need a scout," said Myka.

"And a messenger," said Spring.

Other fairies volunteered—Rosetta, Prilla, Iridessa the light fairy, and even Vidia. One by one, more fairies came forward. Fruit pickers, stonemasons, butterfly herders—no one knew which talents might be needed.

But one fairy fell back. As others came

forward, Silvermist saw Necia turn and fly away. Of course, without a talent, the fire fairy couldn't be any use on the mission. *It's just as well,* Silvermist thought. *We'll have one less thing to worry about without her around.*

Standing at the edge of the fairy circle, Kate saw Necia slinking away, alone. *Poor Necia!* she thought. Kate wondered if she should go after her. She knew Necia didn't have anyone else to talk to.

Mia tapped Kate on the arm. "I think we should volunteer to go see Kyto," she said.

"What? Why?" Kate asked in astonishment. After their last trip to Torth Mountain, she was sure Mia would want to stay as far

away from dragons as possible.

"The fairies have always helped us," Mia said. "Now they need our help. We can't just sit by and do nothing. After all, Pixie Hollow is our home in a way, too."

"Mia's right," Lainey chimed in. "We have to help however we can."

Kate looked at Gabby. "What do you think? Are you up for this?"

Gabby nodded.

"Even if we have to fight a dragon?" Kate asked.

Gabby nodded again.

"Okay," Kate said. This would be their biggest Never Land adventure yet, but she didn't feel excited. She felt scared.

Kate glanced once more toward the Home Tree. Necia had vanished. Into her room, Kate guessed. Necia hadn't started all those fires—the dragon had. If they could defeat the dragon, maybe Necia really could feel at home in Pixie Hollow. Didn't she owe it to her friend to try?

Kate stepped forward and spoke up. "Queen Clarion? We'd like to come, too."

Chapter 13

Kate knelt at the edge of the Wough River. She dipped her hand into the cold, rushing water, then patted her forehead to cool herself off. The journey to Torth Mountain seemed longer than it had the first time. But maybe, Kate thought, that was only because she knew what lay ahead.

Mia, Gabby, and Lainey rested nearby

in the grass. Gabby lay stretched out on the ground with her head in Mia's lap. Mia was stroking her hair. The little girl's face looked pale and exhausted, and Kate wondered if they'd been wrong to bring her along. She was only six years old, after all. Gabby's words about Kyto echoed in Kate's head: *I don't want to see another dragon ever again.*

But they had seen another dragon. And they'd see one again before the day was through.

Kate glanced over to where Queen Clarion, Silvermist, Tink, Myka, and a few other fairies huddled together, discussing strategy. All together, nineteen fairies of different talents had come on the mission to ask for Kyto's help. Back in Pixie Hollow, it had seemed like a strong group. But out here in the open, with Torth Mountain looming ahead, the fairies looked pitifully small. Every time Kate thought of Kyto's evil eyes and fiery breath, she tried not to shake. Were they on a fool's errand?

"Everybody ready?" Tink called to the group. "Let's keep going."

The journeyers slowly picked themselves up and rose into the air. After several more minutes of flying, they arrived at the vertical wall of rock. Carefully, they made their way around the base of the mountain, past boulders and spiny shrubs. When they came to the rock Kate and her friends had hidden behind only days before, the group spread out. It was the queen's idea that they should be less of a target in case Kyto flamed.

Kate crept up to the rock, bracing herself

for another terrifying glimpse of the dragon.

But to her surprise, Kyto didn't seem nearly as frightening as before. He lay on his belly with his head resting on one arm. Kate had the impression that he'd grown smaller.

No, she realized. That wasn't it. It was his hoard that had diminished. The neat piles of treasure were now scattered all over, as if they'd been carelessly thrown about. Kyto had curled his body around it as best he could, but Kate could see gold coins strewn across the ground, out of his reach. Kate guessed almost half the hoard was gone.

The loss seemed to have affected the dragon physically. His skin looked dry. His eyes were dull and glazed.

"Kyto," Myka said, approaching with Queen Clarion at her side.

Kyto didn't even bother raising his head. "You're back, I sssee."

Queen Clarion cleared her throat. "We've seen the new dragon, Kyto, just this afternoon. We know now that you were telling the truth. We've come to ask for your help."

Kyto looked up. A spark of interest came into his eyes. "You're going to unchain me?"

There was a long pause. The queen and Myka exchanged worried glances. "No," Queen Clarion said. "You know we can't do that."

Immediately Kyto's eyes turned red. His lips peeled back from his teeth in a snarl. *He's going to flame!* Kate thought. She prepared to duck.

But the dragon only turned away. "Then we have nothing more to talk about."

The fairies seemed flustered. Kate could tell they were all thinking the same thing. *What do we do now?*

Queen Clarion fluttered a few inches closer and tried again. "Kyto," she said, "it was wrong of us not to believe you. But there must be a way for us to strike a deal. If you can tell us how to defeat the new dragon, we will give you something in return. An item for your hoard—anything you want."

"My hoard?" Kyto snorted, and two little clouds of white smoke steamed up from his nostrils. "My *hoard*? Do you ssssee what has become of my hoard, thankssss to you?" he screeched.

The queen flinched, but she held her ground. "If you help us, we will make sure that every item of your hoard is returned,"

she told him. "*And* we will bring you something new, anything you—"

"QUEEN CLARION!" Myka shouted suddenly. "LOOK OUT!"

A flame screamed through the sky, charring the rocks where the queen had been hovering just seconds before. The girls and the fairies ducked behind their rocks. Circling their heads was the new dragon.

"I'm back for more treasure," the new dragon bellowed. "And I see some little scavengers have followed me here. Perhaps I'm not the only one who's interested in your hoard, Kyto."

Kyto reared up on his hind legs and shot a ball of flame into the sky. "Tyras! Only a coward would steal from another dragon's hoard!"

Tyras? Kate was surprised that Kyto knew the other dragon's name. Why hadn't he told Spring and Myka before?

Tyras swooped down, aiming for a pile of gemstones. Kyto whipped his tail around just in time, smacking the new dragon out of the way.

The fairies scattered. Some hid behind spiny, cactus-like bushes or in patches of scratch grass. Others flew into crevices in the side of the mountain or cowered beneath boulders.

Kate pressed her back flat against the rock she was hiding behind. She looked over at her friends. Lainey had her arms over her head. Mia held Gabby tight against her. Gabby's eyes were squeezed shut and her hands were covering her ears.

A fearsome screech echoed off the rock walls. Kate peeked around the edge of the rock again. She couldn't help it. She just had to look.

Flapping his wings, Tyras tucked her talons to her body and dove headfirst at Kyto's pile. Kyto swiped the air wildly in defense, landing a blow across the other dragon's neck. As the dragons clashed, Kate realized that Tyras was even bigger than Kyto. Her scales were a grayish purple. Her head was more angular, and her teeth were a disgusting yellowish brown. Tyras's heavy tail was lined with sharp, bony plates, which she swung at Kyto.

Kyto was doing his best to defend himself and his hoard, but the chain held him back. For the first time, Kate felt almost sorry for him. When he landed a blow that knocked Tyras sideways, Kate found herself silently rooting for him.

As the battle continued, something glinting on the ground caught Kate's eye. With a jolt of horror, she saw that it was Queen Clarion. The queen was cowering beneath a spindly plant as the battle raged over her. She had been trapped there when Tyras

dove, and now she was afraid to move. Kate realized that if the queen didn't get away, she'd surely be struck.

When Kyto drove Tyras back for a moment, the queen took her chance. She darted away from the plant, heading for a tall crop of boulders. Her crown flashed in the sunlight.

Tyras's head swung around. When she saw the queen's shiny crown, her eyes turned red. She let out a screech and lunged at her.

"No!" Kate screamed.

But it was too late. In an instant, Tyras had snatched the queen in her claws. With a flap of her wings, the dragon rose into the air and was gone.

Chapter 14

Silvermist watched in horror as the dragon flew away with Queen Clarion. She let go of the rock she'd been clinging to and floated down to the ground. One by one, the fairies and girls came out from their hiding spots and gathered together.

"We have to go after them!" Tink cried.

"And then what?" Vidia said. "*Think,* Tink

darling. If we run after that dragon without a plan, we'll be crisped faster than you can say *flambé*."

"You'd rather *leave* the queen with that monster?" Tink exclaimed.

"I'd rather stay alive," Vidia snapped.

"Stop it, you two," Silvermist said. She rubbed her head. Their bickering was making it hard for her to think. "Vidia's right. We need a plan."

They looked at one another in silence.

"Someone must have an idea," Silvermist said. "Anyone?"

"We could release Kyto," Spring said.

"Another dragon?" Prilla whispered.

Everyone turned to look at the dragon. His eyes were closed, and he was breathing hard from the battle.

"No," Tink whispered fiercely. "We agreed before that we wouldn't release him. We don't need two dragons on the loose."

"There's only one way to get your queen back, then," Kyto hissed, as he'd been listening all along. "You'll have to arrange a trade."

"A trade?" Tink asked.

Kyto got heavily to his feet and began gathering up his treasure. Using his tail as a broom, he swept the precious items into a pile. "Sssomething valuable. Sssomething rare. Sssomething any dragon would covet even more than a fairy queen and her crown."

Silvermist found herself staring at the dragon's pile. Was there something in there they could use?

As if he'd read her mind, Kyto's tail suddenly snapped forward, whiplike. The tip

struck right in the center of the fairies. It caught a sparrow man named Orren across the back, sending him flying.

The fairies cried out and fluttered to him. Orren was sprawled on the ground, gasping for air.

Kyto bared his teeth at them. "Touch my hoard, and that'ssss the least of what will happen. I've already helped more than you dessserve. You brought thisss on your-ssselvesss."

The fairies retreated. It was clear Kyto would be no more help to them. Tink threw her hands into the air in frustration. "We need to do something *now*! Spring, Myka, follow that dragon and track her where-abouts. Everyone else, *think*. What can we use for a trade?"

"I know of a rare flower, a silver violet, that only blooms once in a hundred years," Rosetta said. "It grows on an island out in the Sea of Dreams."

"How far away is it?" asked Tink.

"A day's flight, maybe more," Rosetta said.

Vidia shook her head. "Even I'm not that fast."

"What about pearls?" Mia suggested. "We could ask the mermaids for one."

"Too common," Iridessa said. "And we don't want to have to go to the mermaids. They might not help us."

Other fairies suggested things—a rare butterfly, a golden fruit, a beautifully carved rock. But none of these things seemed precious enough to trade for their queen.

"I've got something," Gabby said. She

stepped forward and removed the costume fairy wings from her back. Silvermist had never seen Gabby without those wings. She knew they were her most prized possession. They were only made of fabric and wire and glue—not valuable enough to tempt a dragon. But Silvermist was touched, and she could tell the others were too.

"Keep your wings, Gabby. They're worth

more on you," Kate said. Mia put an arm around Gabby's shoulder and kissed the top of her head.

All this time, Silvermist had been racking her brain. There was something she was forgetting. Something extraordinary, something no one had ever seen before—what was it?

"I know!" she cried suddenly. "We need Necia!"

"You want to trade Necia?" Prilla looked scandalized.

"No, not *trade*," Silvermist said. "I think she can help us!"

"How?" asked Fawn.

"Fire is a dragon's greatest weapon," Silvermist explained. "And Necia understands fire better than anyone. If we can't find a way around Tyras, maybe Necia can."

"She can," Kate spoke up suddenly. "I'm sure of it."

"How do you know?" asked Fawn.

"I—I can't say," Kate told her. "But believe me, there's more to Necia than meets the eye."

Silvermist took one look at Kate and knew her hunch had been right. "I think we've been wrong about Necia—*I've* been wrong," Silvermist admitted. "We have to at least try."

"Do you think she'll come?" asked Tink.

Silvermist hesitated. After all, the fairies of Pixie Hollow hadn't exactly welcomed Necia. Why would she help them now?

"There's only one way to find out," she said.

Chapter 15

Kate sat on the ground, resting her back against a pine on the eastern shore of Never Land. A strong wind whipped her hair around her face as she gazed out at the water. Just offshore, she could see Skull Rock. The great skull-shaped rock jutted up from the waves like a giant rising from the sea. A cavern formed the skull's mouth. When Kate squinted, she could see Tyras's tail sticking out from it like a tongue.

It hadn't taken Myka long to track Tyras and Queen Clarion to the cave. Kate thought it seemed like a fitting place for a dragon to make its lair. This wasn't the first time Kate and her friends had been to Skull Rock. They'd been there once before. They had been looking for a missing fairy. Unfortunately, Skull Rock wasn't any less creepy the second time around.

"What's taking them so long?" asked Lainey, who was sitting next to her.

"Do you think Necia said no?" Mia asked.

"She'll come," Kate said. Still, she wished she'd gone with Silvermist and Vidia to bring Necia back. The fairies had said they could fly faster on their own, and speed was

essential now. But Kate knew that Silvermist
and the fire fairy weren't exactly friends.
What if she couldn't convince her?

Tink flew over to them. She had dimmed
her glow so it couldn't be spotted from far
away. In the gloom of the forest, she wasn't
much brighter than a firefly.

"Hold out your hands," she told the girls.

They did as she asked. Tink placed a little
leaf-pouch in each of their upturned palms.

"What's this for?" Kate asked.

"More fairy dust. We weren't expecting to fly so far today. You should all have a backup supply. You wouldn't want to run out when you're flying over the sea."

Or inside Skull Rock with a dragon, Kate added to herself.

The girls tucked the extra fairy dust in their pockets. But Tink still hovered, tugging at her bangs. Kate had the feeling there was something she wanted to say.

"We should have believed Necia when she said she didn't start that fire in the orchard," Tink said.

Kate knew she'd struggled to find those words. Tink wasn't always one to admit when she was wrong.

"There'll be plenty of time to make it up to

her," Kate said. "First we need to save Queen Clarion."

"Do you think Queen Clarion is safe?" Mia asked, looking out at the cave.

"Tyras must have wanted her for a reason," Tink said. "She wanted her crown, no doubt. A fairy queen herself is rare. If Tyras thinks the queen valuable enough, she'll do anything to protect her."

"Do you think Tyras plans to stay on Never Land for good?" Mia asked.

"It certainly looks like it," Tink said. "She's built up quite a hoard." Piles of treasure surrounded the mouth of the cave. Among the gold and gemstones, Kate saw things she hadn't noticed before—a wooden ship wheel trimmed in gold, a marble statue, something that looked like a giant crystal egg. She wondered if they were all from Kyto's hoard, or if Tyras had plundered other dragons' hoards, too.

"Why do dragons have hoards, anyway?" Gabby asked.

"Because their minds are clever, but their hearts are empty," Tink answered. "They can't love. They have to have something else to live for."

"Do you think there are nice dragons somewhere?" Lainey wondered.

"Maybe," said Tink. "But not that I've met."

The wind was still blowing from offshore, bowing the treetops and rustling the leaves. Faintly, Kate heard a bell-like sound. She jumped to her feet.

Her friends were up, too. "Do you hear that?" Lainey said.

Just then, they glimpsed three spots of light coming through the trees. Vidia and Silvermist were returning—with Necia!

"We're back," Silvermist said. Next to her, Necia nodded, looking determined. "And, Gabby," Silvermist added, "we're going to need those wings of yours after all."

Chapter 16

The flight across the sea to Skull Rock was gusty and turbulent. The girls and their fairy friends struggled through the wind, which seemed to come at them from all sides. It didn't help that they had to travel the long route, flying around the island to approach from behind the cave. It was the only way to stay hidden from the dragon's view.

By the time Kate touched
down, she was shaking. She
took a deep breath to steady
her nerves. The girls and
fairies fanned out around Skull Rock, each
taking their positions. Kate, Gabby, Necia,
and the light fairy Iridessa found a hiding
spot behind a rock near the mouth of the
cave.

"Do you see Queen Clarion?" Iridessa
whispered.

"No," Kate whispered back. "Tyras is in
the way." The dragon's huge body lay across
the entrance.

Kate glanced across the spit of sand to
where Mia and Lainey were hiding behind
a jagged boulder. Could they see any better?
If they could, they gave no sign.

"She must be somewhere inside the cave. We'll have to keep Tyras distracted long enough to go in and search for her," Necia whispered.

Kate nodded. They'd hoped they'd be able to spot the queen right away. It would have made rescuing her much easier.

Then again, she thought, *no one said this would be easy.*

Kate pulled a handful of damp pine needles from her pocket and placed them on the ground. Gabby removed her fairy wings.

Now they had to wait for their cue.

It came a moment later. Out in the water, just beyond the edge of Skull Rock, they saw a tiny light flash—once, twice. It might have been the glimmer of fading sunlight on a wet rock. But Kate knew it was Silvermist

winking her glow to let them know everyone was in place.

This is it. Necia snapped her fingers to
make a spark, then carefully lit the pine
needles. Kate took a deep breath, then blew
a stream of air at the smoldering pine needles. The flames jumped higher. Plumes of
smoke drifted toward the mouth of the cave.

Tyras's head whipped around when she
smelled the smoke. She grunted and got
heavily to her feet. She took a few curious
steps toward the mouth of the cave.

"Your turn," Kate whispered to Gabby.

Gabby held her wings up to the fire and
began to flap them slowly, casting a shadow
on the dark cavern wall. Now it was Iridessa's
turn. She began to shape the shadow, moving the light so that it grew bigger and more

frightening. Together, the little girl and the fairy were making a perfect shadow puppet. With the help of Iridessa's light magic, the shadow of Gabby's fairy wings looked exactly like dragon wings.

Good girl, Gabby! Kate thought. Why had she ever doubted bringing Gabby along? The six-year-old was as brave as any of them!

When she saw the shadow, Tyras's eyes glowed red. "Kyto! Is that you?"

It's working! Kate cheered silently.

Kate added more damp pine needles to the fire, sending up more smoke. She just needed to keep Tyras distracted a little bit longer.

When Tyras's head was turned, Necia darted from their hiding spot and sprinted across the sand toward the cave. At that moment, Kate noticed Mia gesturing wildly from her hiding spot.

"What's she saying?" Kate asked.

Mia mouthed something and pointed at her fist.

Suddenly, Kate saw what was wrong. Tyras's right forefoot was balled into a fist. A faint glow came from between her talons.

Queen Clarion! Kate thought. The queen was caged inside the dragon's claws!

"Necia, stop!" Kate whispered. But it was too late. The fire fairy had already slipped inside the cave.

Kate's heart sank. How would they ever get the queen now?

Just then, the dragon's eyes narrowed. She sniffed the air and hissed, "That's not dragon smoke I smell."

Oh no! Kate thought. Any moment now, she'd come out and find them. The plan was falling apart!

With her nose in the air, Tyras didn't seem to have noticed Necia scurrying past her feet. The fire fairy stopped by Tyras's claw—the same claw that held Queen Clarion.

All of a sudden, Necia waved her hands. A ball of fire whizzed past the dragon's face, close enough to singe her scales. Tyras roared and stumbled backward in surprise. Her talons opened—only for a second, but it was long enough. The queen darted out.

On the other side of the cave, Tink and Vidia sprang from their hiding place to meet her. They took hold of her on either side and pulled her away.

Instantly, Tyras lunged at them. Her jaws closed with a loud *snap!* For an awful moment, Kate thought the dragon had caught them. But a second later, she saw the three flying out of the cave.

Tyras tipped her head back and let out a thunderous roar. It was so loud that Kate had to cover her ears with her hands. She ducked back down and watched as the dragon flapped her wings, rising into the air. Her neck drew back as she prepared to flame.

"Now!" Mia shouted from her hiding spot behind another boulder.

That was the *second* cue.

As the dragon's fiery breath gushed out, Necia darted up to meet it. She held up her hands and the flames curled backward, as if they'd hit an invisible wall.

The dragon jerked back in surprise. She shot another stream of fire at Necia. Once again, the fairy sent it back.

With Necia providing cover, the fairies flew out of their hiding spots. Kate and Gabby dashed across the beach to rejoin Mia and Lainey. Everyone was ready to fly back to shore.

"Come on, Necia!" Kate shouted. "Let's go!"

She looked over her shoulder, expecting to see Necia making a break for it. That was the plan, after all. She only needed to keep the dragon occupied long enough for everyone to escape.

But Necia wasn't coming. She was waging a full-scale battle against Tyras. As the stunned girls and fairies watched, Necia whipped flames into a spinning ball of fire, driving the dragon backward.

"What is she doing?" asked Vidia.

"She's *winning*!" cried Kate.

Necia's fire seemed to be growing stronger and more powerful by the second. Slowly but surely, she was forcing the dragon deeper into the cave.

"Careful, Necia," Mia said under her breath.

Lainey covered her face with her hands. "I can't watch!"

Gabby was squeezing Kate's hand so hard that she couldn't feel her fingers anymore.

The dragon flapped her wings faster. Her tail slashed through the air, snapping forward like a whip. Necia lunged out of the way, but she was too close to the rocks. She slammed into the side of the cave at full speed.

Kate's hands flew to her mouth. She watched in horror as Necia fell through the air and landed on the sand.

"Get up!" Gabby cried.

Necia was lying motionless on the ground. Kate saw a glint  of satisfaction in Tyras's eyes. As the dragon loomed over the fairy, her jaws opened wide. She was going to flame.

She'll burn Necia to a crisp! Kate thought. *Help!*

Chapter 17

Silvermist was watching from her lookout point when she saw Necia fall. She didn't wait to see what Tyras would do. She dove from the rock, stopping in the air just above the surface of the water.

Summoning all her water magic, Silvermist plunged her hands into the waves and flicked her wrists with a sharp snap. A giant wave ripped toward Skull Rock—and crashed right on top of the dragon's head.

Tyras stumbled and fell backward onto her haunches, stunned.

Come on, Necia! Get up! Silvermist cried silently.

From where Silvermist hovered, Necia looked like a small ember in the shadows of the cave. Slowly, Necia pushed herself up to a sitting position. She shook her head and flapped her wings. Her glow burned brighter and deeper. She began to fly toward the mouth of the cave.

Tyras had recovered from the shock of the wave. She started after the fire fairy, fury in her red eyes.

Necia had almost reached the beach, when she suddenly stopped. Then she started to fly *backward.*

"No!" Silvermist yelled. What was she doing? Had she lost her senses?

The other fairies and the girls were screaming to her, too, but Necia didn't seem to hear them. She flew forward again, and this time Silvermist noticed the trail of fire coming from her hands. Necia weaved and darted through the air, directing the fire this way and that. The fire swelled. But it wasn't just getting bigger—it was *transforming.*

Silvermist gasped as the fire grew into an enormous, flaming *fire*-dragon!

Tyras blasted another stream of fire at Necia. But the flames only seemed to feed

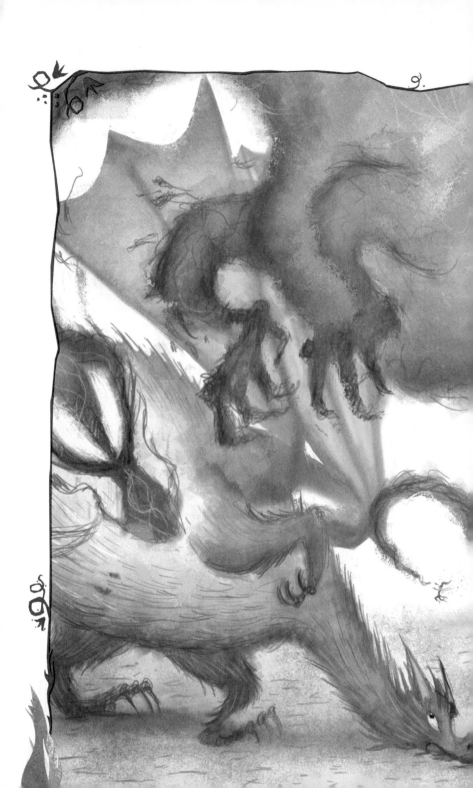

the fire-dragon. Tyras flamed again, and the fire-dragon swelled until it towered over Tyras. Its belly was an inferno. Even from where Silvermist hovered, the roar of the flames was deafening

As the fire creature grew larger, Tyras cowered in terror. Necia waved her hands again, and her fire-dragon spewed a geyser of flames. It seemed to be too much for Tyras.

With a shriek, the dragon flapped her wings and rose into the air. She carved a wide arc through the sky, circled Skull Rock, and headed east toward the horizon. A zap of white light streaked across the sky.

In a blink, the dragon was gone.

As soon as Tyras was out of sight, Necia dropped to the sand. The fire-dragon disappeared, as if it had been suddenly extinguished.

Silvermist flew to the mouth of the cave. She landed next to Necia. "Are you all right?"

Necia looked exhausted. But she managed to nod. "Is he really gone?"

"Yes. For good this time, I think." Silvermist ran her fingers lightly over Necia's wings, checking for tears. When she was sure there were none, she stepped back. "I'd fly backward," she said.

Necia looked startled by the apology. "What for? You saved my life!"

"*You* saved Queen Clarion. You saved everyone. And we doubted you—me most of all," Silvermist admitted.

Necia was quiet. "I thought you just didn't like me," she said at last.

"I know. I wasn't very welcoming when you arrived," Silvermist said. "I think I was afraid of you. I'm a water fairy, after all. Fire is the opposite of what we love most." She gave an apologetic smile. "But even though we have different talents, that doesn't mean we can't be friends." She held out her hand.

Necia smiled and clasped it. "Friends," she agreed.

Silvermist pulled the fire fairy to her feet, then put her arm around Necia's shoulders. Kate, Mia, Lainey, and Gabby came running toward them. The other fairies came out of their hiding spots, too. They were all whooping and clapping.

"That was so *cool*!" Kate exclaimed.

"Did you see the look on that dragon's face?" Tink laughed.

"I've never seen a *dragon* get scared before!" Myka added.

Queen Clarion made her way toward the fire fairy.

"Are you all right, Queen Clarion?" Necia asked.

"Yes, thanks to you." The queen took

Necia's hands in hers. "I underestimated your talent. I had no idea you could control fire like that. And who would have thought of a fire-dragon! Necia, you are truly one of a kind."

Necia's glow turned scarlet red. The queen looked concerned, until she realized the fire fairy was just blushing.

The queen turned and whispered something to Spring, the messenger. Spring nodded and darted away.

"I asked Spring to go ahead to Pixie Hollow and tell the fairies to prepare a feast," Queen Clarion explained when the messenger was gone. "We have a lot to celebrate."

The fairies began shaking the soot and sand off their wings, readying themselves for the flight back.

"Hey!" Gabby said suddenly. She plucked a shiny gold coin from the sand and held it high in the air. "What about this?"

They all looked around. Coins, gems, and other treasures glimmered in the wet sand. The hoard had been scattered everywhere in the battle.

"It belongs to Kyto," Tinker Bell said. "Most of it, anyway."

"I say we leave it," Vidia said. "We don't owe him anything."

"No," Queen Clarion said. "We'll take it back to him."

"Why?" asked Kate. "Kyto didn't help *us* at all."

"Kyto's hoard means everything to him," the queen explained. "And he did try to tell us about Tyras—we just didn't believe him. Even a nasty dragon like Kyto deserves some kindness. Everyone carry back what you can."

The girls and fairies spread out, plucking treasure from the sand. Silvermist and Necia each took half of a thin silver chain. Tink carried a golden ring, and Vidia chose the lightest thing of all—a rainbow-striped feather. Silvermist knew she'd picked it because it wouldn't slow her down.

Gabby was running around grabbing coins and putting them in her pockets. "It's like an Easter egg hunt!" she exclaimed.

Mia passed by with ropes of pearls around her neck. A jewel-encrusted crown sat lopsided on her head. When she saw

Silvermist and Necia staring, she gave a sheepish shrug. "I guess I always wanted to be queen for a day."

"Not me," Necia said.

"Me neither," said Silvermist.

They looked at each other across the silver chain and smiled. Silvermist knew they were both thinking the same thing—it was good just to be a Never fairy.

Chapter 18

That night at the fairy circle, the celebration was in full swing. Music talents played almond-shell lutes and straw flutes as fairies danced through the air. Firefly lanterns hung from the branches of the surrounding trees.

But the circle was even brighter than usual, thanks to the tiny fires Necia had lit all around it, each one carefully contained in a seashell.

Kate popped a roasted chestnut in her mouth and munched with contentment. "This is the best arrival party I've ever been to," she said.

Beside her, Mia laughed. "This is the *only* arrival party we've been to."

"When are you guys going to take that stuff off?" Kate asked her friends. Mia, Lainey, and Gabby were still wearing the crowns, necklaces, and other jewelry they'd found in Kyto's hoard.

"Oh, Kate. Let us have fun for now," Mia said. "Kyto's going to get it all back tomorrow." The fairies were planning to return the hoard first thing the next morning.

"I wish I could see his face when they

bring it to him," Kate said. It was hard for her to imagine Kyto looking happy.

"*I* don't," Mia replied. "If I never see a dragon again, I'll be just fine."

Lainey leaned over and nudged them. "Look at Necia," she whispered.

Necia sat next to Silvermist in the center of the fairy circle. The fire fairy's dark eyes shone as she watched the party swirl around her. She looked happier than Kate had seen her since she'd first arrived in Pixie Hollow.

"She finally got what she deserves," Mia said.

"That's right," Kate said. "A celebration."

At that moment, Queen Clarion floated forward. She held up a hand, signaling the musicians for quiet.

"Today is a great day for Pixie Hollow,"

the queen said. "We honor the arrival of a new fairy—it is long overdue." She turned to Necia. "Your bravery saved me, and it saved Pixie Hollow. Your talent is rare and wonderful. That's why I hereby lift the ban on your fire-making. From now on, you are free to practice your talent wherever you like—except in Dulcie's kitchen," she added with a wink.

All the fairies laughed. Necia laughed hardest of all.

"Enjoy the party," the queen said. "Tonight is a night for celebrating."

As the music started again, Kate heard a soft thump. She looked over and saw that Gabby had fallen asleep against Mia's arm. The day's events had finally worn the little girl out.

"I guess that means it's time for us to go home," Mia said. She stood, then woke Gabby and helped her to her feet.

Gabby blinked. "Did I miss anything?"

"No, Gabby," Kate said. "You were awake for all the good stuff."

"Good." Gabby smiled drowsily and leaned against her older sister.

Mia and Lainey took off the jewelry and

placed it in a pile. "It really is a shame that it's all going to a dragon," Mia said with a sigh.

"I guess," Kate said. "But I actually feel sorry for him. He's alone. I wouldn't trade my friends for all the treasure in the world."

"Me neither," said Lainey.

"Me neither," said Mia, giving both their hands a squeeze.

Kate took a last look around the fairy circle. She wanted to say good-bye to Necia. But she didn't want to interrupt the celebration. *Anyway,* Kate thought, *we'll be back again.*

But just as they stepped away from the circle, Kate heard the whir of wings.

Necia fluttered up and landed gently on her shoulder.

"You believed in me," Necia whispered.

"Even when no one else did. You're a good friend."

"So are you," Kate said.

"Will you come back to Pixie Hollow soon?" Necia asked.

"We always do," Kate said with a laugh. She looked over at Mia, Lainey, and Gabby. They were skipping through the grass, toward Havendish Stream. They couldn't stay away for long. Never Land was too full of magic.

As she walked to the secret portal in the old hollow tree, Kate looked over her shoulder one last time. Silvermist and Necia were flying through

the air together, their arms around each other's shoulders.

Who would've thought that a fire fairy and a water fairy could be such good friends? Kate thought. Smiling to herself, she stepped through the portal to go home.

The next morning, Kate stood by her mailbox waiting for her friends to arrive so they could walk to school together. She tilted her chin to the sky, enjoying the sun on her face. It had rained overnight, and the air felt fresh and clear.

Kate had the feeling she always had when she returned from an adventure in Never

Land. It was the feeling of having woken from a long, pleasant dream. Sometimes that made home seem boring, but not today. As she looked around, the gray sidewalk, the dewy lawns, even the old white mailbox all somehow seemed bright and new.

Kate looked across the street at the Johnsons' house. How many times had she bounded up those steps to show them a picture she'd made at school, or her Halloween costume, or just to say hello? The Johnsons had exclaimed over every picture, every costume. No matter what, they always made her feel special. Kate smiled at the memory. The Johnsons had been great neighbors—the best, actually. They were the kind of people who made her street a good place to live.

It's funny how I met Necia right after the John-

sons moved away, Kate mused. She'd lost some friends and gained another. Maybe change wasn't always so bad after all.

A single new blossom had opened on the azalea bush. It looked bright and hopeful in the morning sunlight. Kate stared at the flower, and suddenly, she knew what she had to do.

When Lainey, Mia, and Gabby rounded the corner, they found Kate picking flowers from the border around her own yard.

"What are you doing?" Mia asked as they walked up.

Kate held up the little bouquet of pink and yellow flowers.

"There's something I have to do really quick," she said. "Come with me."

Together Kate and her friends walked

across the street. Mia, Lainey, and Gabby waited on the sidewalk as Kate climbed the familiar steps of the Johnsons' old house.

She shook her bangs out of her eyes and took a deep breath. If the fairies could make room for Necia, she thought, then she could certainly make room in her heart for some new neighbors.

Kate rang the doorbell. A moment later, the woman she had seen blowing bubbles opened the door. She was holding her baby on her hip. She looked a little surprised to see Kate standing there. "Yes?" she said.

Kate held out the flowers. "Hi," she said. "I'm Kate from across the street. I just wanted to welcome you to the neighborhood."